UNLUCKY in Love

AJ RENEE

Sydney,
   It was great meeting you
at work! Happy Reading!

❤
AJRenee

DEDICATION

To all of you searching for your true love, may you find the love you deserve.

CHapTer 1

"How many fucking frogs do I have to kiss?" I snap and fall on the couch.

Val raises her glass of wine out of the way, and I steal it. I close my eyes as the large gulp I've taken runs down my throat.

"That's mine!"

I glare at her before taking another sip and handing it back. "Thanks."

Leaning my head against the back of the couch, I sigh. I despise dating. I'm over it. Why can't I find my Mr. Right, so we can start our lives together?

Val wraps her arm around my shoulder and pulls me to her. I lay my head on her and stare at the TV, not really paying attention to whatever she's watching.

"What happened, honey?"

"Everything. Nothing," I whisper, exhausted from another emotional roller coaster. "I'm just over it all. All these fuckers," I say, raising my locked phone. "All they want is a quick hookup. Which, sure I could see the appeal if they didn't show up in popped collars or hopped up on 'roids."

I decided to start dating again two months ago. At first, I sat back and observed the wink emojis and messages that came through the app. Tonight, I relented to coffee with Tristan. We'd chatted daily for about a week, so I figured why not? I mean, he was cute and seemed nice.

"What was wrong with this one?" Val asks as she mutes the TV. "Did he not look like his picture?"

I sigh. "No, he matched the picture, dimples and all. He's cute—not hard to look at him."

"So what happened?"

"I arrived a few minutes early and found a table in the corner. I've been reading the book you suggested, so I wanted to finish it. I figured it would help me relax. Tristan got there about five minutes late. Not a biggie since I was reading. He spotted me and asked what I was drinking before buying me another one." I lift my head and smile at Val. "It was really sweet." Placing my head back on her shoulder, I continue. "We sat and chatted for about an hour. He told me a little about growing up in California, and I told him about growing up here in Vegas. You know, all the simple get-to-know-you things we hadn't already talked about yet. He heard my stomach growl. It was so embarrassing, Val. Anyway, he suggested we go to the diner around the corner. I was having a nice time with him, so why not?"

"Everything sounds like it was going great for a first date," Val said.

I nod. "It was. Tristan asked for a booth and slid in next to me. You know, like those old-timey movies? Having him so close made me nervous in a good kind of way. I liked what I was seeing from him, so feeling his body next to mine was great."

"Until?" Val asks, sensing I'm beating around the bush.

"Until after our meal when his hand landed on my thigh."

"Oh?"

"Yup, it surprised me; you know, moving a little fast. But my creeper alarm wasn't going off. When I didn't say anything, he turned and kissed me. It was an overall good first kiss. Sweet, not pushy, no slobber. You name it." I sigh. "He ends the kiss and wraps his arm around me, which was okay. We talked a little more and then he kisses me again." I can't say the words. Anger bubbles up, and I jump to my feet. "Ugh!"

"Izzy, what the hell happened?" Val asks, leaning forward, her forehead creasing with worry.

I meet her eyes. Val is my best friend, and I love her like she's a blood relative. She has always been there when I needed her, and right now is one of those times.

"But then, well—then his other hand inched up toward my crotch and he said, 'Let's go to the bathroom and fuck.'"

Val sends me a blank stare and blinks. "Let's go to the bathroom and fuck?"

I nod.

"And you told him what?"

"Well, at first I was in shock. Nothing at all in the three hours with him led me to believe he was an asshole who was just trying to get in my pants."

Val clucks her tongue. "Oh, young grasshopper... Every guy wants into a woman's pants. The good ones and the bad ones."

"You're not wrong. I guess it just took me by surprise. One minute we were sharing a sweet kiss after talking about favorite movies, and the next it was 'let's fuck.'" I cross my arms under my breasts. "I told him to go in first and I'd follow, so no one would suspect anything. After he disappeared down the hall, I got my shit and left."

"Good girl! Although, he could have used a good kick to the balls."

I laugh. Val is a great friend. She always finds a way to ease my mind. Sometimes it's with a hug and stern talking-to or like now with a good laugh. "Thanks for listening. I'm going to go wash off the dirty boy from my skin."

"Don't forget to Listerine your mouth. I can only imagine how many other women he's pulled that shit with."

Covering my mouth, I fake gag. Val is not wrong, and that's my first order of business. Moving to my room to gather my stuff, my phone vibrates—again. It started about ten minutes after I hightailed it out of the diner. At first, Tristan sounded confused and worried, but his latest text sends a shiver down my body. Thinking about it a little more, I'm happy he showed his true colors early on. I just hope I won't have a wart by the end of my search for Mr. Right.

***

Pouring milk into my mug, I watch the black and white colors swirl together until they turn a pretty caramel. I didn't sleep well, and the creamy mix is exactly what the doctor ordered. Hurrying, I flick the sugar packet and dump its contents. The door behind me opens as I toss the spoon into the sink and lift the mug to my lips. The satisfying liquid warms my insides, and I can't help my sigh even if I tried.

"Rough night?" a velvety voice asks.

I take another sip of my glorious cup of joe before turning toward Mario. He started working in the

Reference Department three months ago and has featured in a few of my dirty dreams. He's gorgeous and about six feet three inches. Dark, tall, and handsome would describe him to a T. I shrug and force my mind from the gutter. He brushes past me and grabs the spoon I just discarded. The first time I saw him do this, I yelped in protest, but it seemed he really was another gross college guy.

One with full kissable lips.

"You're quiet this morning," he says and leans against the counter next to me.

After the episode with Tristan last night, I can't help but stare a second longer. "No, just a date." The words spill from my mouth. "I mean, I was up late."

Mario's mug freezes halfway to his lips, and an eyebrow raises as he stares at me.

"Fuck!" I slap a hand over my mouth in horror. My heart races, and I know my cheeks are bright pink. "I gotta go." I squealed and run out of the break room.

Great job, Izzy! Now he thinks you were up all night fucking.

Calling myself a string of insults, I take the elevator down to the copy office. See, we both work in our college library in different departments. I keep the copy machines and printers stocked with paper and toner, and Mario does whatever the students in Reference do.

We both tend to be in the break room grabbing coffee in the mornings at the same time. If I'm lucky, I get a glimpse of him when I do my rounds. Our conversations aren't long, usually revolving around our mutual love of coffee. His doesn't include milk, but his love of coffee runs as deep as mine.

I walk around the corner and sigh with relief when I find the door closed. My boss, Jerry, isn't in yet, and I know he'll tease me if he spots the blush still on my cheeks. Jerry is old enough to be my dad and is the best boss I've had, not that there have been many.

Kicking the doorstop under the wooden door, I prop it open. I set my mug on the long counter and take a quick peek at the staplers and empty the pencil sharpener set out for students to pop in and use. My body goes into autopilot, and Mario's lips come to mind. I wonder if they are they as soft as they look?

I reluctantly remind myself he's out of my league. It's not that I don't think I'm pretty. I am, but I'm not the girl all the boys come sniffing around. They'll look in my direction, but few take the next step. Of those who do, none are as handsome as Mario.

"Hey, Izzy!" Jerry says, and the swinging half door separating us from the students who come in for help slams shut behind him.

My eyes dart to the side, and my heart races. "Geez! You scared the crap out of me!"

Jerry squints a fraction. "Sorry, I thought you heard me. Are you okay?"

The blush on my cheeks crawls down my neck to the top of my chest. Thank God I'm not wearing a spaghetti strap today or someone would be able to see it. "Yeah, I'm fine. I was just thinking about a paper."

"Some paper," Jerry says. "Go ahead and work on it. I need to go upstairs to admin. I'll check the machines on my way back down. If no one comes in, you'll have a solid thirty minutes of work."

I nod and watch him leave as quickly as he arrived. Instead of working on a nonexistent paper, I put on some music and pull out my phone. Searching through the dating app, I check out the men the algorithm picked for me.

When I'm about to give up and set my phone aside, one man stands out. He's definitely athletic. I wonder if he goes to the gym on campus or if he happens to be a graduate. Scrolling past his superficial stats of six feet three inches tall and brown eyes, I see he works in construction. Noticing we have a few things in common—other than the obvious fact that I like hot men and he's a hot man—I press the flirty wink icon and set my phone aside.

The rest of my day is normal. I work my hours and go to my classes. Later that night, I set aside my laptop and grab my phone. I find a few texts from Tristan. After a quick thanks-but-no-thanks text, I delete him from my phone.

"I'm beat!" Val says and plops across the end of my bed.

"Want some ice cream?"

At the magic words, she's up and I'm following her out of my room. Val sits at the bar while I rummage around, grabbing ingredients for sundaes.

"How was your day?" she asks.

Scooping vanilla ice cream into my bowl, I shrug. "Same ole', same ole'. Although, Tristan—the guy from last night—doesn't seem to get it."

"Don't skimp on peanuts tonight," she tells me when I scoop rocky road into her bowl.

"I never do!"

"Are you going to try again on the app? I don't know how you're doing it. It kind of weirds me out," Val says, holding up her head in her hand.

I laugh. "Val, I've told you about the creeps I've come across working at the library. At least with an app I can sort through them. Maybe I shouldn't do any dates until I've talked to them longer?" I mumble the latter to myself.

I put Val's sundae next to her and grab spoons. My phone vibrates on the counter as I savor my first bite.

Vanilla, hot fudge, and peanuts. All I need to satisfy my sweet tooth.

"Who's that?" Val asks, nodding toward my phone.

"Don't know," I tell her around the spoon in my mouth. With a few swipes of my thumb, I pull up the notification and stare. My lips tip up, and I grab the spoon before it falls from my mouth. "Oh!"

Val jumps down from her seat as I stare at the message.

Johnny23: Hi, beautiful!

"Hello, gorgeous! On the other hand, maybe I should join this Lucky in Love dating site too." Val squeaks. "Who's this guy? This isn't Tristan; I remember how Pretty Boy looked. This guy makes me think of some great, rough sex. Mmmm..."

I laugh. "How long has it been since you've had sex?"

Val shrugs. "I've got some cobwebs a man like *that* could remedy."

My phone vibrates again, and I find another message from the hottie.

Johnny23: Finding your wink after a long day in the sun was just what the doctor ordered.

I giggle at the cheesy text.

Val grabs my phone and shakes her head. "And... that right there is why I have cobwebs." She sighs dramatically as she hands my phone back. "So much potential and then *poof* it's all gone."

Johnny23: Shit, that sounded corny. I won't blame you if you don't reply. Just wanted to say I like your profile and think you're beautiful. It was a nice surprise to find your wink tonight. Have a great life!

Biting my lower lip, I read his messages one more time. It seems the sexy construction worker is as good at dating as I am.

Izzy_Rae: Hi! That was pretty corny. Good thing you sound sweet.

"Oh, Lord. She liked it," Val mutters and takes another bite of her sundae.

I grab my bowl and walk toward the living room. "Come on, let's find something to watch."

CHaPTer 2

Val nods toward my phone. "When are you going to meet this one?"

I smile. "Well, our schedules haven't lined up at all. I actually just gave him my number, so we could talk over the phone."

It's been over a week of messaging each other through the dating app. Johnny has been really sweet, but we haven't been able to go out on a proper date. It frustrates me because I want an in-person gut reaction to the man. The one thing I hate about this online dating shit is never being able to get a real read on the person.

"Earth to Izzy!" Val calls out as she waves a hand in my face.

"Sorry, what?"

"I asked you to tell me about him, but then you went off into Izzyland." Val puts her hand on her hip and gives me her stink eye. She's about to grill me if I don't give her something.

"Johnny's a middle child and has two sisters. He moved here from Phoenix. His favorite show is *Game of Thrones*—"

Val raised her hand. "Stop, before you read me his entire dating bio. Why haven't you been able to meet up? Why is he using a dating app if he looks like *that*? No offense to you, although I still think you can find a guy the normal way."

I cross my arms over my chest and remind myself I love my best friend and she means well. "Valerie! Plenty of people find love through online dating. I haven't been on there for more than a few weeks yet. And I just started talking to him a week ago. What kind of information do you expect me to know about him? Blood type? Who he lost his virginity to? His mother's maiden name?"

"Well, that information would be useful when the cops are searching for you." She shrugs, and all my bluster is gone as a giggle escapes my lips.

Pushing my fingers through my hair, I sigh. "For the record, you didn't know any of that shit when you met up with Kenny the first time, and he didn't kill you."

"No, but he might as well have," Val whispered.

I wrap Val in my arms and kiss her cheek. "Oh, honey, I'm sorry." Kenny and Valerie dated for almost two years before she learned he was not only stepping out on her but gave her an STD. Her body may have healed, but her heart was still in shreds.

Val pulls back and forces a smile. "I'm only trying to look out for you."

"I know—" My phone rings in my back pocket, and I wave a hand.

"Get it."

"No, this is more important. Do you want to veg out and watch a movie or go grab a drink?"

"Nuh uh, who's calling? Is it him?"

One look at my phone, and I'm grinning.

"Go talk to the hottie," she tells me as she accepts the call on my behalf before walking down the hall toward her room.

***

Johnny and I talked on the phone for three hours that night. A record in my opinion. Men aren't universally known for enjoying phone time. He was sweet and listened to my stories as we shared more about ourselves. Johnny works long hours occasionally, and he has a few more weeks of it coming up. I really want to meet him in person to get my feelers out on him, but I will have to settle on listening to his sexy voice.

Lost in my thoughts, I round a corner on my way back to the copy office and slam into what feels like a wall.

"Whoa, you okay?" Mario asks. His warm hands cup my arms as he steadies me.

Checking myself for injuries, I forget about the two reams of paper I was holding. "Ow!" I yelp when one strikes my big toe. Hopping on one foot, I mutter a slew of curses and freeze at the sound of his deep chuckle.

"Really? You're laughing at me?"

Mario straightens, and all traces of humor vanish. "I'm sorry. Izzy, are you okay?" he asks as he cups my elbow, helping me balance in the process.

"No thanks to you," I mumble before seeing his sincere concern. "Sorry, I guess I should pay better attention when I'm doing my rounds."

I look at the two packages of paper on the floor, but before I can pick them up, Mario hands them to me. "Here you go. I better go find these books for Hal."

Hugging the reams of paper to my chest, I watch Mario walk away. He's incredibly attractive and completely out of my league. A sigh slips from my lips as I stare at his bubble butt. His jeans fit snugly around it before loosening at his thighs. His body shifts, and a deep blush fills my cheeks when I meet his eyes. Caught by Mario in the process of checking him out, I turn quickly and hightail it back to the office. All thoughts of Johnny push aside as I bite the insides of my cheeks.

"You okay?" Jerry asks when I toss the reams of paper onto the cart before dropping into my seat.

I wiggle my toe and sigh. "Yeah. I bumped into Mario and dropped one of those damn reams on my toe."

From the corner of my eye, I see Jerry shake his head and smile. He leans forward, and I point my toe toward him. "It doesn't look bruised, and you can wiggle it. I think you'll survive."

"Thanks, Doc."

The rest of my shift goes like any other day. Thankfully there weren't many students coming in, and Jerry helped those who did. This gave me time to put finishing touches on my paper and study for my test later that afternoon.

After waving to those working at the circulation desk, I walk out into the scorching Vegas heat. My limbs slowly defrost after sitting in the cold AC for the last few hours. I flip through my index cards as I walk toward the Student Union. Thanks to my sore toe and the worry I'll bump into another person, it takes me longer than I want.

I grab a quick bite inside from one of the vendors and find a shady spot for a nap. The best part of being on campus is all the people-watching I get to do. It lets me relax and wonder about the complete strangers.

Speaking of strangers, my phone vibrates, and I smile at Johnny's name.

"Hello." I cringe at my husky tone that comes out.

Silence follows, so I pull the phone away to verify I'm still in a call. "Johnny?"

He clears his throat. "Yeah. Hey—hey, Izzy!"

"You okay?" My nerves buzz at the way his voice catches. Sure, I haven't known him long, but he sounds different. Aroused even.

"Sorry, yeah. Damn, babe... You can't answer the phone like that." Babe?

"Like what?" I ask and lean back on my free hand.

"Sexy. It makes me want to know what you're wearing," he chokes out.

My eyes move down my body to the leggings and cute top I'm wearing and smile. "Oh, you know... It's hot outside, so I'm sunbathing topless." What the hell, Izzy?

A deep groan sounds into my ear. "*Fuck!* I bet that's not true, but that image... Wowzer."

The power of his words emboldens me, and before I can stop myself, I ask, "And what does that image do to you?"

"I'm rock hard just thinking about you topless," he says, his voice now husky.

Looking around, I see I have inadvertently picked the best spot away from bystanders. For a moment, I war with the turn in the conversation. I know it's my fault and I should stop it, but I can't help myself. "Is that so? Tell me, big guy, what are *you* wearing?"

I bite my lip to stop a nervous giggle from escaping. My heart races, and I warm from the scandalous conversation. I've had phone sex before with guys I've dated, but Johnny and I have never even met. It's obviously been way too long since I've enjoyed a man's company.

"Babe, you're killing me. I'm painfully hard, and I need to get out of the truck in a second. I don't need these guys staring at the bulge in my pants."

My lips turn down in a pout he can't see. I know it's for the best, and at least one of us is thinking straight. I'm outside in public for goodness' sakes. "Sorry—"

"Don't be. I liked it… a lot. So much I'd love to try again later tonight if you're up for it?" Johnny asks.

Say no. You barely know him. "Sure. You're going into work now?" For a moment, I wonder what must be wrong with me, but a girl has needs.

"Yeah, I was calling to tell you I can't stop thinking about you. I don't think I've enjoyed talking to a woman so much."

He's good looking *and* sweet. I know I have a stupid grin on my face from his comment. "I had a great time talking to you too."

"Talk to you tonight. I need to go will this hard-on away."

"I'm sorry!"

"I'm not. Later, babe."

Staring at the leaves above me, I drop my hand holding the phone to my side. I'm not sure phone sex this early in a relationship is a good idea, but keeping things safe is my trademark. A little adventure will do me good.

***

Contrary to my bold bravado a couple days ago, I've kept my conversations with Johnny rated PG. He's passionate about his work, and at first, I enjoyed hearing about it. I've never known someone who worked in construction before Johnny. Ultimately, he plans to work his way up and own his own company, one that specializes in home building. I love his drive and desire to accomplish it. However, lately when he mentions work, my eyes glaze over. I'm relieved he hasn't noticed it. It's not that I don't enjoy talking with him, I just don't have a lot to add to a conversation about construction. Outside of that particular topic, our chats have been pleasant.

I wave at the supervisor in Circulation and leave the library. My phone vibrates in my pocket. Part of me hopes it is Johnny, but instead I find a notification on the dating app. I haven't opened it since Johnny and I switched to SMS messages.

Eric47: Hey, beautiful! Looking for someone to warm your bed?

"Ugh!" I groan and delete the message before moving to the next.

Barry_365: Hey, gorgeous! How would you like me to take your temperature?

I shake my head. "What the hell?" After I scroll through and delete a few more, I stop.

Andy_7: Hi! I'm new to this app and came across your profile. I'd love to meet up for drinks.

My thumb swipes the screen on its own, and I become engrossed in learning about Andy. Every few seconds I look up, making sure I stay on the path. If I've received this many messages since I started talking to Johnny, how many more has he received? We are only in the getting-to-know-you stage, but the thought makes me curious.

As if on cue, my phone vibrates, and a message from Johnny pops up. I grin, excited to hear from him.

Johnny: How does paintballing and lunch sound for next Saturday?

Izzy: I've never done it.

Johnny: Really? I'll have to be the first guy to take you!

I think about it for a moment. I did tell myself to find more adventures in life. Paintballing would fit the bill…

and it can't be all that hard, right? Plus, I'd finally get to spend time with him.

Izzy: Okay.

Johnny: Great! Can't wait to talk to you tonight! Gotta go!

"I'm paintballing next Saturday?" I mumble before reminding myself it will be an adventure. Something tells me adventure and Johnny go hand in hand. I bite my lip with anticipation. What other things will he have up his sleeve?

A shadow catches my eyes, and I stumble, but I'm able to catch myself. Looking up, amused eyes stare back at me. I can't help but smile as my cheeks burn with embarrassment.

"Hi," I whisper at the same time an annoyed voice snaps, "Watch where you're going!"

My eyes leave Mario's and land on a woman who's a few inches shorter than me. And here I thought I was short. Her curly, dirty-blonde hair comes to her chin, and her hard, green eyes stare daggers at me.

"You okay?" Mario asks, ignoring the woman at his side.

I nod. My eyes flit back and forth, and I realize for the first time that Mario has a girlfriend. A short, spitfire of a girlfriend. "Yeah, sorry about that."

She pulls on him, and they go in the direction I came from. I can't help but watch them walk away. Both are attractive, but in those three seconds, I can't help but feel they are nothing alike.

Mario surprises me when he looks over his shoulder and smiles at me. The blush on my cheeks deepens further at being caught staring. Noticing his attention is not on her, the woman tugs on his arm after narrowing her eyes on me.

I'm not sure what it was all about, but I do know it's

not my business. He's been a gentleman with me until this point, and I don't imagine he's the type to stray. Then again, I don't really know him, so who knows?

CHAPTER 3

The first night we had phone sex, I faked it. I was too embarrassed to touch myself while he talked dirty to me. We said good night, and I slipped out of my clothes, the sound of Johnny's voice fresh in my mind. I put the right amount of pressure on my clit and came hard.

"You want me to lick your clit?" Johnny asks, his voice husky.

I nod and squirm on my bed. It's been so long since a guy has gone down on me, and the thought alone makes my heart race. "Yes," I whisper into the phone.

"Then you better straddle my face and grab onto the headboard," he tells me, and I moan at the mental image.

Since that night, we've talked about our fantasies. When I told him I've never been on a man's face, he scoffed. I must admit I want... no, need to try it out.

Initially, I find the position rather intimate, almost too much. But his words are enough for me to find my clit and rub it furiously.

Now I know how much he enjoys it when I tell him what I want to do to him. I mean, it isn't hard thinking about the body he's sent pictures of. I'm sure plenty of women would drool over Johnny if he stood shirtless on a street corner.

"I love this position because I can play with your nipples," he says, bringing me back from my thoughts.

"Tonight, I'm going to face your feet," I whisper and smile at the deep groan vibrating through the phone.

"What are you going to do while I eat you out?" His breath is uneven.

I bite my lip and imagine taking him in my mouth while he takes his time pleasuring me. "What do you want me to do?" I ask, unable to say the words.

"Lick it, lick my cock. Swirl that pretty pink tongue around the tip and run it down my shaft to my balls." He pants.

"And after I lick it?" My body tightens with my impending release.

"Take me as far as you can and suck me off. I want to come in your mouth so bad." He continues to pant, and I can tell he's close.

Not a minute later, we are both moaning as we come. I listen to our heavy breaths, my body lax from the orgasm, before I hear rustling from Johnny's end of the line.

"I know we decided on no actual sex the day we meet, but I won't be able to stop thinking about tonight when I finally get to see you," he whispers. "Falling asleep, babe."

"Night, Johnny."

"Night," he says, and the line goes dead.

I lie in bed and stare at the ceiling. Johnny's been a sweetheart and a gentleman. When we talked seriously about phone sex—not just flirting with the idea—he didn't balk when I told him it didn't guarantee the real deal. The last thing I want is to lead him on.

My gut still needs to meet him. The texts, phone sex,

and conversations are only leading up to whether we will make a good match. For all I know, he could be a sociopath. "Nobody's got time for that," I mutter to myself.

***

A voice clears, and I look from the textbook that has occupied most of my morning into a pair of pretty, green eyes.

"It's jammed." He shrugs and lifts the stapler chained to the desk.

I smile and walk around the desk to him. He's not much taller than me and has a nicely toned body. I glance at him when I pick up the stapler, and he smiles, exposing two dimples. Forcing my eyes down, I go through the routine of trying to unjam the damn thing. It happens more than it should, and I've reminded Jerry to order a new one a few times now.

"Sorry, this happens a few times a day," I mumble.

He shifts closer to me, and my palms begin to sweat. I'm not sure what he's doing, but I'll never know because Jerry comes in and asks, "Jammed again?"

"Yeah. We really need to get a new one," I tell Jerry, stepping half a foot away from the cute guy.

"Here, let me," Jerry says and steps between us, and I'm trapped between the two desks.

I peek at the guy and notice his slight frown as he watches Jerry work.

"There you go!"

"Thanks," the guy mumbles, and I follow Jerry back around the large counter.

"Can you close tomorrow night? Chris had something come up," he says, mentioning one of the other students who work in the office.

I watch the cute guy slip out with slumped shoulders and sigh. "Yeah, that's fine. I can come in after my class."

"Great! I appreciate it," he tells me and turns to his computer.

With my eyes on the words in front of me, I think back to the cute stranger. Even if Jerry hadn't walked in then, I don't know if the stranger would have said anything. Plus, if he did, I'm already talking to Johnny. I'm not comfortable dating more than one guy at a time. I briefly wonder if Johnny is seeing other girls before I shove the thought aside. I hope he isn't, but it isn't like we've even met in person.

It seems ever since I decided to start dating via the app, I've run into good-looking guys everywhere. Just this morning, a guy who could have easily been on the football team flirted with me.

Closing my eyes, I remember the way his dark skin formed around his biceps. "Are you taking Dr. Wilson's class?" he asked with a nod toward my textbook.

Only, I zeroed in on his sexy, full lips. As if on cue, he wet them, one side lifting in a smirk. He noticed the way I was staring, and I smiled stupidly before nodding.

"I took it last semester. If you'd like, I can help you with the work."

I curled my fingers around my book to stop myself from fanning my face. The way he watched me suggested studying was the last thing he was thinking about.

The desk vibrates and scatters the memory aside. After unlocking my phone, I stare at the message.

Jerry: Earth to Izzy. The guy already left the office.

"What?" I say and swivel in my chair.

Jerry laughs as he leans back in his seat. "Well hello, Izzy!"

"What are you talking about?"

"You zoned out after the guy left. Should I go find him, so you two can exchange numbers?" Jerry tells me, and I know he's crazy enough to do it.

"No! That was nothing!" I say, and my face drains of color when Jerry gets up and walks toward the door.

"Jerry! What are you doing?" I squeak.

Jerry laughs. "I need to go to admin. I'll be back later."

I'm not sure how long it takes me to calm down. Jerry loves to tease, and he has no issue embarrassing me. I guess it's because he's known me since I was in eighth grade.

Izzy: You suck, and you're the worst boss in the whole world!

Jerry: Ha. Ha. Ha.

CHAPTer 4

"I can't wait to see you later!" Johnny says.

My face pulls tight with a large smile. "I'm looking forward to it too." My stomach flips around a few times, but I'm not going to tell him that. "I'll see you later!" I tell him and hang up.

I'm excited and nervous for today. Either this will go great and we'll continue seeing each other, or it will blow up in my face and Val will have to notify the authorities I'm missing. While it's a farfetched thought, I know it's a possibility.

The next few hours drag along until I finally make my way to the paintball location Johnny texted me. Only a few cars are in the lot when I arrive. The sun is beaming down on me through the windshield, cooking me little by little through the thick glass. After a few minutes idling, the heat is no match for my car's AC, and I shut the engine off.

"If he doesn't show up in the next five minutes, I'm out," I mumble to myself as I stand in the sliver of shade provided by a single palm tree. It's ninety-nine degrees outside, and I'm wearing camo I bought at the army surplus store on the crappy side of town. My skin is about to melt off my flesh and bones. I could remove this jacket but then I'd risk a sunburn. A lose-lose situation in my book.

The sun reflects off the windshield of an oncoming truck and temporarily blinds me. Looking through spots, I manage a quick peek at my phone and verify the truck matches the description Johnny sent me.

"Hey, babe!" Johnny says as he saunters over.

I must admit the man is sexier in person than I imagined. His broad shoulders taper into a slim waist, and his pants fit snugly around his large thighs. My lady bits stand at attention, and I'm pleased to note they're on board for this date—this long overdue date.

"Hi," I say from my shaded spot.

"Wow, you're hotter than your pictures!" Johnny gathers me into his very muscular body for a hug, his firm muscles wrapping around my soft body.

I smile up at him as he puts me on my feet. "Thanks, you're not so bad yourself."

"Come on, this is going to be so much fun!" He steps back and grabs my hand. With a tug, he pulls me in the direction of a small trailer. "I still can't believe you've never been paintballing before."

I shrug, but he doesn't notice as he's too busy dragging me along. The man is nearly a foot taller than me. Normally, this level of enthusiasm is something I like in a man, but each step he takes is two of mine. He told me how much he loved paintballing, but I didn't understand until this moment how excited he is to share this with me.

We haven't even paid for our entry, and I'm hot, sweaty, and winded. I wonder if I should have talked him into a different place for our first date. I look up at the black, long-sleeved T-shirt covering Johnny's broad back and remember the sexy pictures he sent me over the last two weeks.

Get your shit together, Izzy.

It took quite a bit for our schedules to line up for today. I figured a date in broad daylight would keep me in check. It's not that I think sleeping with Johnny is a bad idea, but I'm trying to make sure I don't let my body make the decisions. At least not on the first date.

Don't get me wrong; I'm no prude either. Johnny and I have enjoyed some hot phone sex. The man knows how to get a girl going with only his voice—a huge plus in my book—and it's also given me some great sex dreams. It's also left me vibrating with the urge to jump his bones, hence my need for a date in broad daylight.

My thoughts scatter when I slam into Johnny. Heat floods my face as I look around. While I disappeared into La-La Land, he guided me into the air-conditioned trailer.

"You okay, babe?" his deep voice asks, and my thighs clench together.

"Yeah, I'm so sorry!" I squeal.

Deep brown eyes stare into mine with an intensity I didn't expect. I freeze when his large hands tilt my head back. "I've been wanting to kiss you for-fucking-ever," he whispers.

My eyes flutter shut when his warm lips press against mine. His fingers find my hips and dig into my flesh. I sigh, and his tongue slips into my mouth. Everything about it is the epitome of a great first kiss. I grab onto his shoulders, enjoying the sweet assault. Our kiss deepens, and the world around us floats away. I no longer remember my annoyance that he was twenty minutes late. Or even the fact we are in a very public place.

Johnny growls, and my eyes pop open the moment his tongue thrusts awkwardly into my mouth. What the hell? Gone is the sexy, sweet kiss from not even a second ago. In its place is... a disastrous inexperienced kiss. Confusion clouds my mind at this change of events.

Releasing his shoulders, I run my hands between us to his chest and begin to push back, and someone clears their throat. I remember where we are, and I know my cheeks are inflamed for the second time in ten minutes. Thankfully, Johnny also hears the noise and unravels his tongue from my poor tonsils.

"Sorry, I lost control." He gives me a boyish smile before he turns and speaks with the young attendant who is also blushing.

I'm grateful for the moment to compose myself. And by compose myself, I mean wipe my damn mouth. I replay the kiss and try to understand how it went from a smooth kiss that set my body on fire to a messy and slobbery one.

"Is that good with you, babe?" Johnny asks, but I have no idea what he's talking about. The attendant looks at me expectedly before summarizing something that still doesn't make any sense.

"Um, yeah. Sure, that's fine."

Twenty minutes later, I'm standing with all the paintball equipment I've been given, including a facemask. The staff and Johnny are adamant this mask stay on my face during every moment of field time. I want to keep my eyeballs, so I don't argue with them.

"Teams, take your places!" a referee calls out from somewhere to my right.

I lift my hand and grab the mask to pull it down, but Johnny grabs my wrist.

"Kiss me good luck!"

I'm hesitant at first. His wet kiss is still on my skin, and I'm forcing myself not to cringe. Only, I never do. This kiss is like the beginning of the first. It's sweet. It makes me want more, and it's far too short.

Johnny puts my mask in place and then his own. The buzzer sounds, and I can honestly say the next hour flies by. I will also admit… I suck. I should be embarrassed by how badly I played. Sure, it was my first time playing, and I should give myself some slack, but I was *really* bad.

Johnny, on the other hand, is a beast on the field. For having such a large body, he was agile in his movements. The other team struggled to shoot him. The times they did manage to was because he was busy trying to keep me alive. The other players on our team gave up early on and opted for saving their own asses.

I hurt everywhere. Even my ear hurts from being grazed by a paintball. I need a hot bubble bath to soak my aching body.

"We should grab a bite to eat," Johnny suggests.

Looking down at my now-neon-camo outfit, my nose scrunches with displeasure. "Food sounds great, but I stink."

"Did you bring an extra set of clothes like I suggested?" Johnny asks as we walk the last couple feet to my car.

I chuckle. "I did, but all I can do is smell how stinky I am. No set of clean clothes is going to change that."

"How about you follow me back to my place? It's not too far, and you can wash up there before we grab some food."

With a charming smile directed at me, it's hard to say no. Before I can give him my answer, my nerves bounce around as his lips brush mine. My nipples push against the tank top I'm wearing under the camo. Each swipe of his tongue stirs my desire and leaves me wanting more. My thighs quiver with need, and I lean into him, tasting his lips. Salty and sweet, he draws me in farther into his embrace.

I wrap my arms around his shoulders, and he lifts me off the ground. His prodding erection presses against my stomach. Maybe following him back to his place won't be such a bad thing. Daylight date be damned. My sore legs lift on their own and wrap around his slender waist. Johnny groans into my mouth and forces his tongue across mine.

I stiffen. Not far from my mind is the way our first kiss ended. His large hands grab my ass and pull me flush to him. My core throbs at the friction, wanting what lies just behind our clothes. He ends our kiss and presses his forehead against mine. Our heavy breaths mix as we try to calm ourselves.

"We better go... If you're up for it?" His voice is raspy and reflects the same desire pulsing through my body. I lower my legs and slide down the front of his body.

"Sure," I say with a smile. "Why not?" I find my keys and unlock my car. Johnny opens my door and waits as I throw a sheet over my seat, another of his suggestions, and remove the camo top suffocating me. He kisses me on the head and shuts the door. The chivalrous act surprises me, and I watch him as he makes his way across the parking lot to his truck.

Johnny wasn't lying when he said he didn't live too far from the paintball field. Seeing how good he is, I wouldn't put it past him to be a regular there. I grab the bag with my spare clothes and look up at the apartment building.

Last minute, I shoot Val a text letting her know where I am and who I'm with. My instincts are only questioning this guy's kissing skills, not whether he's a homicidal maniac. But I still opt to stay on the side of caution.

"Ready?" Johnny asks, and I put my hand in his waiting hand.

Every step I take is killing me. As time passes, the soreness only settles deeper in my body. I look up, hoping this is the last flight of stairs and try to ignore the pain radiating from each spot I was shot. How anyone thinks being shot repeatedly is fun is beyond me.

"This is me," Johnny says and flashes me a brilliant smile.

Within seconds, we are on the other side of the door, and I'm taking it all in. The apartment is the epitome of a bachelor pad. It has minimal furniture but tons of electronics. I can't see the kitchen from where I'm standing, but I do kind of wonder if there are pizza boxes and beer there.

Johnny blocks my view and steps closer to me. I tip my head back and look into the chocolate-colored depths of his eyes. The details of his apartment disappear into the far recesses of my mind. Awareness tingles along my skin at his nearness.

"One kiss, and I won't bother you as you clean up," he whispers.

My gaze falls to his mouth, and my tongue runs along my lips. "Mhmm," I mumble as I wrap my arms around his neck.

Johnny gathers me and brings our bodies flush against each other. My hard nipples press through the fabric of my shirt as they seek his chest, now barely covered in a white wife-beater.

His body reminds me of men I see in magazines. No, really. I'm still shocked *he* contacted *me*. He's not some meathead, but his body is sculpted. I know he goes to the gym, but these muscles are carved from the long hours at his job.

His lips graze the skin of my neck, stopping all forms

of thought. The trail of kisses along my skin causes goose bumps to erupt across my body. I let my neck fall to the side, giving him more access and secretly hoping he doesn't stop. It's as if he hears my silent plea and takes his time exploring.

Each nibble is soothed with a kiss, and his hands take their time massaging my ass—the only part of my body not sore from the ass whooping I got. I run my fingers through his short hair, enjoying the texture against my skin.

"You're incredible," he murmurs, and the puff of air against my sensitized skin makes me moan.

I squeeze my thighs together to stave off the pressure building in my core. It's becoming nearly impossible not to squirm under his touch. One of his hands cups me, and my head falls back, my mouth open wide at the delicious friction.

So much for daylight helping me stay in check.

"You're making me crazy," he confesses before covering my mouth with his.

I nip at his lower lip, and he groans. He freezes for a second before I'm pushed backward against the door. Lost with desire, I tilt my head hoping to deepen our kiss, and Johnny follows my lead.

I'm needy and rub against his hand, looking for some sort of friction to put me out of my misery. The thick bulge in his pants pokes at me, and I envision running my hand down, following the thick vein on his dick. Emboldened by the fantasy, I press my hand over the fabric covering his erection.

Johnny snaps under my touch, and our kiss deepens. I have power over this man. I'm making him crazy. I'm undoing his control. I'm—going to choke on his tongue.

What the hell is going on?

My eyes pop open as they begin to tear up. Johnny's

eyes are closed, and he moans into my mouth. I recoil at the force of his kiss, no longer eager and ready for him. Gone is the hot-as-fuck, rip-my-clothes-off kisser, and in his place is the inexperienced man who's about to drown me. It's like a switch just flipped.

What do I do?

In my state of shock and disgust, everything hits me at once. A whiff of our mixed-together sweat is so far from sexy that my nose crinkles in response. The only thing I hear is the swapping of spit in my mouth. I'm no longer an active participant in what had been a toe-curling kiss.

I can't do this anymore. He's not letting up, and it's become obvious when this man loses control it becomes a slobber fest. With my back against the door, I slide my hands down to his chest and push.

The sound of Val's ringtone fills the space around us, and I nearly weep with relief.

"Call them back," Johnny whispers against my lips. My tonsils are finally free from his assault, and I take the opportunity to turn away before he takes my poor mouth again.

I lie. "I'm sorry. I can't. It's my mom, and I've been waiting for this call."

Slipping from his hold, I fumble and grab my cell phone. "Mom? Is everything okay?"

"No, no it's not, Izzy!" Val snaps into my ear. "What is wron—"

"Okay, I'm on my way!" I tell her and hang up. I barely glance at Johnny as I grab my bag from the floor. "I'm so sorry, but I have to go!"

"Is everything okay?"

No, you almost suffocated me with your kiss. "I don't know, but she needs me there now."

I open the door and take a step, but his voice stops

me. "Here, let me walk you to your car at least."

The idea of another kiss has me scrambling. "No, it's okay. Thanks for everything!" At the last word, I hurry toward the stairs. Every bump and bruise makes itself known as I take them two at a time.

I manage to get to my apartment complex without killing myself. Looking up at the two flights of stairs, I groan. When I make it to the top, I insert my key, but the door opens before I can unlock it.

"Seriously, Izzy? What is wrong with you? You barely know the guy! You didn't tell me you were going over there until last minute! Why did you lie and say I was your mom?" Question after question comes tumbling out of Val as she interrogates me.

Walking past her, I head for my room where I drop my bag on the bed and grab my towel. She follows me to the bathroom door where I turn to face her. "I will tell you everything, but *please*, I need a hot shower first."

When I close the door in her face, Val slaps her hand on it and stops me. "Did he hurt you?"

My smile doesn't reach my eyes. "No, but I'm sure I hurt him."

The hot water is divine on my achy body. I examine myself and find fifteen bruises and a few more spots I expect to follow close behind. After towel-drying my hair, I wrap it around me and go to my room.

Val lifts her head, and her eyes round. "What the hell happened to you?"

After spending five minutes staring at my body, I know what she sees. "I *suck* at paintballing."

"Paintballing?" she asks, and her brows draw together for a second. "Oh shit, that's right! I forgot you guys were going paintballing."

I nod and search through my drawer for clean underwear and a bra. I pull on my underwear, then release the towel as I sit on the end of my bed, keeping my back to Val.

"Oh shit, Izzy!"

I look over my shoulder as I slip on my bra. "I told you I sucked. I'm one big fat bruise." After I dress, I crawl onto my bed and drop next to her.

"Wow…" Val says after I recount my date, beginning to end. She turns onto her side. "What are you going to tell him?"

"I don't know. He's a nice guy, Val. Hot damn is he sexy, but I just can't. I know I sound superficial, but I can't get past how ugly those kisses got. I hate the idea of hurting him. He really is a nice guy, but—I just don't want to settle."

"Well, take a nap for now and then tackle it. He's been blowing up your phone, so I'm sure he realizes you lied and ran. For what it's worth, I don't think you're being superficial. Superficial is staying with him only because he's hot as sin, regardless of his tongue lashing." Val laughs and kisses my head before leaving me to my thoughts.

CHapTer 5

"This one can't be as bad as the last one," I tell Val, who's looking at me with disbelief.

"Izzy, you were black and blue for two weeks," she says as her eyes bug out.

"Well, there was that."

"And you nearly choked."

I nearly did. A shudder runs through me at the memory. "Look, I am going to be late, Mom."

"Don't you 'mom' me, young lady!" she snaps, and we burst into a fit of giggles.

I know Val is only looking after me during this online dating chapter of my life. I'm hoping to find my prince in this vat of slobber. My last date may have been sweet as can be and hot as hell, but it didn't go as I'd hoped.

Oh, well. You live and learn.

With a quick wave behind me, I hurry and get into my car to meet Brad. I've been chatting with him online and via text for nearly three days. Val waves from the curb, but as I drive away, I see she's already looking at her phone. Tracking me, to be precise. Her father is a retired cop, and she's as protective as a bear. And I love her for it.

Twenty minutes later, I arrive at the small, Italian, family-owned restaurant. It didn't matter how many times I told Val I wasn't nervous. My nerves are still shot. Meeting someone new is hard.

I've dated guys I met the normal way and the now "new" norm of online dating. It's a toss-up whether I'll have a love life again. Going through the dating scene isn't always fun. I remember liking it once... long ago.

My ex and I were together for a couple years, so when we split, I wanted my freedom. I was fine with it just being me and my vibrator. Now? Now I'm ready to give this shit a shot again. The problem is after Johnny and Tristan, I'm not feeling very confident.

Inside the restaurant, I look at the tables and see the moment he notices me. Brad is wearing a lime-green bow tie, and a small part of me cringes. Luckily, his style is something I can overlook.

"Can I help you, ma'am?" the hostess asks.

I shake my head and point toward the man, now standing by his table, before I walk into the dining room.

"Hi, beautiful!"

"Hi," I tell him as he plants a chaste kiss on my cheek.

Brad pushes my chair in behind me like a gentleman. "Thanks for meeting me tonight."

"Thanks for asking," I say on autopilot, and my cheeks warm. This is always so damn awkward at first. At least with Johnny it wasn't so bad. We'd spent quite a bit of time on the phone. Sure, some of it was spent telling each other naughty things, but whatever. The level of awkwardness wasn't bad, at least not until the kisses.

"Izzy?" Brad asks, and I realize I missed whatever he just said.

"Sorry—" Damn this date has me lost in thought already.

"Don't be. First dates are always hard." He chuckles, and the sound soothes me. "I asked if you've ever been here before."

"No, I haven't. I've driven by here a million times though." I open the menu and try to school my features as I read the selections. For being a small, quaint place, the prices are highway robbery.

"Oh, great! I'm going to order us the osso buco! It's amazing!" Brad says. He removes the menu from my hands before I can even see what it is.

I smile politely and lift my glass of water to my lips. I am not a fan of men who take over like that, especially when we barely know each other. My eyes flit toward the door. *Stay positive,* I repeat to myself.

"White or red?" Brad asks as a waiter walks toward our table.

I'm tempted to ask for a shot of tequila, but I don't. "White is fine—"

"You know, a pinot noir would go better with the *vitello*." His statement is more for the waiter, and I wonder why he even bothered asking me. My hand on my lap balls into a fist. I swear it feels like an hour has gone by when it's really only been twenty or thirty seconds. I force my fingers open and fiddle with the napkin on my lap, urging my sweat glands to calm the hell down.

"How many dates have you been on with Lucky in Love?" he asks of the dating app.

"Not many," I say and look down at my lap for a moment. "How about you?" I force the words, knowing I need to give the guy a shot.

"A few months," he admits with a goofy smile.

The awkwardness is only thickening around us with

these few sentences. I'm determined to see this date through, but a voice in my head tells me there won't be a second one. When the waiter shows with a bottle of wine, I breathe deeply, thankful for the reinforcements.

"Would you like a glass or the bottle?" the waiter asks Brad.

"Leave the bottle," Brad tells him with only a cursory glance at the label before placing our order.

I don't object as I mentally calculate how many glasses I'll need to stop this painful process.

A blonde walks by, and my date undresses her with his eyes. After the woman disappears, he looks at me. "I'm glad you agreed to meeting me here."

"Yeah, I—"

"Oh, man, the osso buco," he says, emphasizing his statement with an exaggerated lick of his lips. "I have been thinking about it all day."

I can only stare because I am so repulsed. Here I thought he was going to mention his excitement over meeting me, but no. Whatever the osso buco is has his complete attention, lip smacking to boot. Not to mention the number of times he's asked me something only to interrupt me.

"Where would you like to go after dinner?" he asks, his eyes trained somewhere behind me.

Crap. I haven't spent ten minutes with this man. I'm not sure I even want to finish this meal, which hasn't been ordered, let alone discuss after-dinner plans.

"Oh... I—" I exhale, relieved when the server shows with warm bread and olive oil.

He tells us about the mix of seasonings and pours oil on top. It gives me just enough time to think of a reply.

"Oh! This looks good. I'm famished," I say and grab a roll. "I saw *The Notebook* is playing for this month's free movie in front of Town Hall." Please don't want to watch it.

"Oh… yeah—um, sure. If you want?" he says, pain reflecting on his face.

I plaster a smile onto mine. "Great!"

"Do you like to golf?"

The look of horror on my face matches his from a moment ago. "Um… no?"

"Really? You don't sound very sure," he says, and I'm tempted to throw the roll in my hand at his head.

"No, I don't play. We were more of a baseball-watching family."

"Baseball?" he sneers, as if he stepped in a pile of shit.

"Yeah, you know the sport with the bat?" I snap. I should have kept my mouth shut, but his look of disdain hit a nerve.

His eyes flash briefly before he dawns a mask of civility. The quickness catches my breath, and a shiver of unease runs down my spine.

"I'm quite aware of the sport. How about tennis?" he asks and raises his wine glass to his lips.

Thankfully, the waiter walks up then, preventing me from needing to answer him with another "no."

"You're in for a real treat tonight. The osso buco by Chef Antonio is an award-winning entree." The waiter tells us with so much delight, I wonder if he's being sincere or faking it until he makes it.

A plate is put in front of me, and I will admit it's pretty. Some sort of meat sits next to creamy potatoes, and extra-large asparagus spears add color to the variation. I look up and watch Brad dive in without a word. His lips wrap around the fork, and his eyes roll back. I wonder for a moment if this man is shooting a load into his trousers. He's got total O-face going on, and it isn't attractive on this guy.

At least Johnny was hot as fuck. Sure, he couldn't kiss worth a damn, but I could stare at him all day long. Brad, on the other hand, not so much. Looks aren't everything, and I know that, but he's lacking in that department, and his personality leaves something to be desired.

I haven't felt comfortable the entire time with this man. Not a I-think-he's-going-to-murder-me kind of uncomfortable. More like the we-don't-have-a-damn-thing-in-common-so-why-did-I-agree-to-this type.

My stomach growls, pulling me from my thoughts, and I decide to enjoy the pretty meal. I cut into the meat and try not to cringe when I see it's pink. I'm more of a well-done, let's-not-moo-about-this kind of girl. I swallow back my upset and cut off a piece of the darker meat.

The meat melts in my mouth. I'll give this one to Brad; he chose well. I try to push the fact aside and eat. Brad seems to finally shut up now that he has *his precious* in front of him. This change in direction brings me relief. No more tennis or golf talk. I kind of expected him to ask how my 401(k) was doing.

Not good at all if he's wondering. I mean, come on. I'm a student and working in a copy office on campus.

I scoop up another bite and check out the crowd around us. It's a varying group of guests tonight. My eyes stop and focus. I'm pretty sure I am seeing the corner of an MC's cut near a far wall. A woman to my left a few tables down looks like she's addicted to her Botox shots. To my right is a man a few years younger than us, trying to woo his girl.

Then there's Brad and me in the middle of it all. I can't even call it a blind date. I wish I would have seen the signs during our first couple conversations. I guess I did, but I chalked it up to jitters from chatting with a new guy.

I was wrong.

"Everything okay?" Brad asks before gulping the rest of his wine.

I stare at him, trying not to ask him the same question. He literally drank half of his glass of wine in one sip, for lack of a better word. "Yeah, I'm fine. Why?"

"You stopped eating," he tells me, and I glance between our plates. He has about three bites left, and I've probably eaten a quarter of my meal.

I'm running out of cooked meat, and even though my stomach is ready for more, I'm going to have to claim I'm full. I hold back a deep sigh at the thought. "Yeah, it's good. What is this meat? It's so tender."

"Veal."

My stomach cramps down hard at the meaning of the word.

"Isn't it delicious?" he says before digging into what is left on his plate.

"Oh… okay," I manage to say. Damn, damn, damn. I'm no vegetarian or vegan, but I was better off not knowing that fact. Now I can't pry the image of those big, sad, brown eyes of a calf from my mind. Way to ruin my food, Brad! I mentally whack this man upside the head.

Seeing him lose himself in his meal once more, I decide I'll focus on the asparagus and potatoes. When I peek up between bites, I note he's swallowed his last forkful and is staring at the remnants on his plate.

If he licks his plate, I'm out of here.

He pours more wine into his glass and sits back. I mentally prepare myself for more questions but watch his eyes darken with lust at a different woman passing our table. I can appreciate she has one hell of a body, but this man has no manners.

Spotting the last roll in the basket, I make a grab for it. I break off a piece, and it's halfway to my mouth when Brad decides to open his mouth again.

"Are you sure you should be eating more bread?"

I contemplate throwing my steak knife at him for about half a second. No, orange jumpsuits are not flattering on any size woman. I pop the delicious bread into my mouth, hoping I can pulverize it and alleviate the raw desire to do the same to this punk ass.

"It's delicious," I reply with a forced smile.

He nods slowly at me before he scoots back. He drains his glass and stands. "If you'll excuse me a second, I need to use the men's room."

I smile and give a quick wave of my fingers, seeing I have bread in my mouth once more and I wasn't raised in a barn. Brad walks in the direction I came from, and the unease I've been experiencing since arriving goes with him.

"Not a chance in hell am I doing this again," I mumble quietly.

Enjoying the solitude, I allow myself to relax as I finish off the roll he deemed me too fat for. Sure, he didn't say those words, but he meant them nonetheless. I hope he's in the bathroom with the squirts.

I spot the waiter and wave him over. I'm ready for this night to be done, and I might as well ask for a to-go box. There's a chance Val will eat the baby on my plate even if I can't stomach the idea.

The man scurries off, and I lean back in my chair with my glass of wine. People-watching is better than any soap opera on TV. I love to guess the background of people before me. I note movement in the back and smile when I see the biker.

Tall, dark, and handsome fits the man to a T. There is a hint of danger around him. I watch his eyes move to the beauty at his side and soften a fraction. I sigh and gulp down the last of my wine. The warmth spreads through me, and I know better than to drink more.

A few minutes later, the waiter returns with the box and the bill. With a place as classy as this, I'm a bit surprised to see it return before Brad does. Then again, my date has been gone for quite some time.

"Sir?" I say, stopping the man before he retreats to help his next guests.

"Yes, ma'am?" he asks, and I watch his face blanch a fraction.

"My dinner companion? You don't happen to know if he's still in the restroom?" I see the answer before I can finish my question. The man shakes his head before running off to his next table.

I'm not sure if I should be relieved I don't have to see Brad again or pissed he dumped me with the check. Relief. That's what I'll focus on.

I pull my credit card from my purse and grab the bill sitting on the edge of the table. I've never had an issue with paying the tab or doing my part on dates. Although, Brad ditching me like this is pretty insolent behavior.

After flipping the black folder open, I stick my card in and glance at the total. I freeze as it shuts and open it once more. "Shit…" I murmur to myself before adding "I hope your dick falls off."

It seems Brad has expensive tastes. My face is flushed with not only embarrassment but anger. I force my manners to lead me through this clusterfuck. I got through signing the bill and asking to have the bottle recorked with a small smile on my face. Carrying the bag of leftovers to my car, I consider how many ways I would love to beat the shit out of Brad.

Needing to vent, I call Val.

"Hey, girl! Everything okay, or is this one trying to

drown you too?" She chuckles.

"Want to bring your shovel?" I ask, my voice sounding strange even to my own ears.

I hear Val rustle around, and the noise around her dies down. "Oh, yeah. What happened? Do I need to bail you out?"

"Four hundred and fifty-two dollars and eighty-eight cents."

"Hmm, I always thought bail would cost more. Okay, I'm on my way," Val says without a second thought.

"No." I point my car toward home. My body shakes with a fierce anger. "I'm not in jail."

"Okay… What is the four hundred and—"

"That is how much I just paid for dinner." I tell her through clenched teeth.

"What?" Val yells.

"Yup. You see, Brad…" I spat his name. "He decided he would order for me. He also chose an almost three-hundred-dollar bottle of wine. Then the fucker walked out after enjoying a glass and a half and nearly licking his plate clean."

"What a bastard!"

I smile for the first time in hours hearing her say that. "So now I'm on my way to the apartment. You and I are going to drink every fucking drop of this wine that better have gold in it."

"Aye aye, captain!"

"And, Val?"

"Yeah, honey?"

"You get to pick the next one. If not, you *will* be bailing my ass out of jail," I say and hang up.

I hope Brad the Chump chokes on his next veal meal. I refuse to let this punk ass stop me from finding Mr. Right. I am, however, not unopposed to making a voodoo doll to teach the bastard a lesson.

CHAPTER 6

"Oh, look. How about this one?" Val asks, shoving my phone in my direction.

I glance down and nod. "He's cute. What else?"

"He likes comedies and action movies. He graduated last year. He likes to golf—"

"No!" I snap, memories of Brad still fresh on my mind.

"Is that a dating profile?"

I freeze at the familiar deep voice before looking up into Mario's eyes. He smiles, amusement written all over his handsome face.

"No!" I say at the same time Val tells him, "Yes." I stare at her in horror before looking between them. The food court in the student union is bustling, but I can't hear anything past the rushing blood in my ears.

"Why'd you stop? Someone's going to get the table!" a whiney voice tells Mario.

I watch a flick of annoyance cross his eyes before he looks at the woman. It's the same one I nearly ran into on my way to the car the other day. His lips pull back into an apologetic smile before he walks away without saying another word.

"Whoa," Val whispers loud enough for me to hear. "Why are you on this site when you know *him*?"

Shaking my head, I force my eyes to my food. "Is there anyone else who has caught your eye?" I ask, forcing the conversation back to the search for my prince.

"Uh-uh... Who is *that* guy? Tell me about him first. You've never mentioned a sexy Latin god." Val leans forward, and I know she's found Mario in the crowd. "You realize he's staring at you, right?"

It takes all my willpower not to look in his direction. "Val, he clearly has a girlfriend. He's not available, and you're wrong; he's not interested. He is only entertained by my use of a dating app."

"Whatever you say," she mumbles and sits back to search the app.

I squirm in my seat when the sensation that I'm being watched becomes too much. With a stretch, I look around the food court and finally bring my attention to Mario. His eyes meet mine before he winks and returns his attention to his girl.

"Told you he's been watching," Val mutters and leans toward me with the phone. "Okay, this one. I think he's a good choice."

***

"That's fancy for a night in," Val says, nodding toward the outfit I pulled from my closet.

"Well, I'm going out."

Valerie looks at me, and her eyes narrow before she looks around the room for a moment and looks right back. "Where are you going?"

I sigh. "I'm going to have drinks with a guy."

"What guy? The one I picked out?"

My eyes shift around, and I sigh. "No?"

"What do you mean, 'no?'" she asks as her hands go to her hips. "I thought the next guy would be picked by *moi*?"

"He was, then this guy popped up, and he wanted to meet for drinks. I figured, why not?" I smile, hoping to appease her.

"Why not? Girl, you have some shitty-ass luck picking men. That's *why*." Val shakes her head slowly and releases an exasperated sigh. "Who is he?" Her fingers wave me on. "Come on. Spill the beans, so I at least can guide the cops in the right direction when we have to find your chopped-up body."

I raise my brow. "Dramatic much?"

Val stares at me, and after a minute I shrug.

"Well, I wasn't sure if I would even say yes to him. He's a single dad and has two kids. He says his ex-wife is batshit crazy."

I grab the purple dress I laid out on my bed and remove my pants. Val crosses her arms, clearly upset I'm giving another guy a shot.

"What do you want me to say? I can't give up. I refuse to give up on love. There's got to be a guy out there for me, right?"

"Sure, but don't come to me when you meet a guy who puts Marilyn Manson to shame."

My lips tip in a smirk. I know Val is only concerned for my well-being, and I love her more for it. "I don't think it'll ever get that bad. At least I hope it doesn't. Can you zip up the dress for me, please?" I ask and give her my back.

She kisses my cheek when she's done and turns me around before she grabs my shoulders. "Look, I just want to keep you safe."

"Yes, Mom. I know I haven't picked great guys. Although, other than Johnny not being able to kiss, he wasn't so bad." I smile. "He was actually a sweetheart."

"So sweet, he was going to drown you—"

"Oh, stop it, Valerie. I should have kept my trap shut about his kissing. Look, I'm going to meet Robert. We'll be at the café on Fifth Street. You can sit in your car and watch if you'd like, but I hope you don't. It's going to be fine. I'll let you know when I'm heading home, okay?" The words are meant to soothe her, but I'm reminding myself just the same.

After hugging her, I walk away and head to the bathroom to apply lip gloss and eyeliner. Once I'm satisfied with the simple touch-up, I grab my purse and head to my car. I'm nervous of the upcoming meeting. Those other guys didn't work out, but like I told her, I refuse to give up on love. I have faith love is around the corner. It must be. I just can't be that unlucky, can I?

When my car is finally parked, I drop my keys in my lap and wipe my sweaty hands on my dress. I'm freaking out on the inside. I close my eyes and take a deep breath. Once my heart slows, I force myself to leave the car and head inside. The only person I see sitting by themselves is an older woman.

I order a hot chocolate. I normally grab one on campus, but this café has a tasty one too, great for this time of day. I find a seat and sit with my back against the wall, so I can watch the front door. A few minutes pass before I see a man who looks an awful lot like Robert walk in. He looks around the nearly empty café and smiles when his eyes meet mine. He's handsome and dressed casually for our date. His body is softer than most guys closer to my age, but I can tell he still takes care of himself. When he walks the last few feet, I try to take in as much as I can, noting he looks a bit older than the thirty-two he told me.

Pushing to my feet, I offer my hand.

"So nice to meet you," he says. He ignores my hand and kisses my cheek. "I see you already got your drink. Let me go order mine." He smiles and walks away.

Sitting down, I watch as he glances at me a few times. His beautiful smile causes my face to warm. My internal alarms are alert, but nothing about Robert makes me want to grab my drink and run. I hope this doesn't blow up in my face.

"I'm really glad you decided to meet me tonight," he says as he sits in the chair across from me.

"I'm glad you asked! Have you been on Lucky in Love very long?" I ask.

"No, just a few months. How about yourself?" he asks and brings his cup to his lips.

"Not long. You mentioned you have two little boys?"

His eyes brighten. "I do. They're seven and eleven years old."

This is my first time seeing a man with kids. "Have you and their mom been separated long?" When Robert stares into his cup, I wonder if I've pushed too hard too fast. "I'm sorry, I—"

"No, you're fine. She's still in their lives. You mentioned you're a student?"

I nod. "I'm working on my MBA."

He leans in, visibly interested. "You can do a lot of things with an MBA. What do you want to do?"

I laugh. "You're right. I can, but I have no idea what I want to do. My bachelors is in hotel management because I liked the idea of working in a casino, but now I don't know. I'm a bit burnt out at this point." I shrug before sipping my drink.

"I understand that."

"What do you do?" I ask.

He waves a hand as if to say nothing exciting. "I work security."

I laugh. "That sounds like it could be interesting."

He nods. "Tell me about it. Although, now I pull more day shifts where people are better behaved. When I worked nights, there was no telling what would happen."

"I bet."

"So I have to ask. How is a beautiful woman like yourself on Lucky in Love?"

I shrug. "I was tired of being single, and I wanted control over the choosing process, I guess."

"That just tells me the guys in your life are idiots. Their loss is my gain," he says with a wink. While his words are sweet, I wonder if he's just piling it on too thick. Johnny had corny lines too, but Robert's seem forced.

"Why are you on Lucky? You mentioned your ex is crazy, but that doesn't say much." I know I'm pushing the heavy topic early on, but I'm curious. He's already mentioned her mental state, so I figure it's a safe topic.

"I guess, much like yourself, I was tired of being lonely." Robert puts his crossed arms on the table and leans toward me. "What kind of things do you like to do?"

"I know it sounds lame, but I love to read, see shows, and go to the movies."

Robert nods as he listens to me. His eyes dip to my chest every few minutes but not in a creepy way. He's nice looking, but I must be honest with myself. There's no spark between us.

The least I can do is be polite and see this one to the end.

"What do you like to do?" I ask.

"I like going to the movies and seeing comedy shows. I also like extreme sports. Hang gliding is next on my list." He smiles, and it brightens his face. I can tell he gets excited over this part of his life.

"Oh, wow! That is... crazy. I don't know if I could ever go hang gliding. I'm a bit of a wuss. What other things have you done?" I ask, genuinely interested in this world even if it's not something I'd do personally.

He chuckles. "Yeah, my wife hates it too. I've gone skydiving, white water rafting, snowboarding, skiing, and bungy jumping. I'm also teaching my boys how to skateboard and do tricks on their bikes—a constant sore spot for their mother."

I notice his present tense of his use of "wife" but figure it's still a fresh separation. "Last time I stepped on a skateboard, I face-planted. I did learn rather recently I can't go paintballing either." I lift my shirt a little and show my faded bruises.

Robert licks his lips. "When did that happen?"

"Almost two weeks ago? I'm sure another day or two and there will be no trace of them. I suck at paintballing." I laugh at the memory. I was bruised and battered those first few days. If I wasn't so susceptible to bruising, there wouldn't be a sign of them at this point.

"Wow, that's crazy. I'm a bit of an adrenaline junky, but I've never had bruises last that long," he says with a nod toward my midsection.

"Growing up, it was awful. My shins were always black and blue. I guess that's why I've stuck to more calm activities. Although, I'm waiting for the day I give myself a black eye with my tablet."

Robert looks at me strangely, and I realize I'll have to elaborate.

"I read in bed, and many times, I start falling asleep and the tablet slips from my hands. One day, I expect it will hit me just right."

He nods, and I see I'm losing him. "What kind of

crazy things do you see at work?"

"You name it, and I've probably seen it." He laughs.

I say the first thing that pops in my head. "Clowns?"

He covers his mouth as he mulls it over. "A few years back, there was a clown convention—"

"Clown convention?" I ask and know my eyes are round with surprise. I guess there really is a convention for just about everything.

He chuckles. "Yeah, I can't even make this shit up. So imagine tons of bright colors, painted faces, and wigs. I swear they were everywhere. Anyhow, I was doing my rounds, and I heard this weird giggle coming from an employee-only hall. No one should have been in there, so I opened the door and froze."

"What?" I ask, engulfed with the need to know what happened next.

He shakes his head. "I found two clowns fucking."

"Nuh uh!" I giggle.

"That's not even the kicker because I've come across a lot of people going at it. Every time he pumped into her, they would both giggle. Like this creepy giggle. Pump. Giggle. Pump. Giggle."

I burst into a fit of laughter at the image. Covering my mouth with my hand, I sit back. My body shakes as I imagine two clowns with their bright red pants around their ankles. "You—are—making this up!"

"Nope. They didn't even notice me standing there. I cleared my throat a couple times before giving up and walking away."

"What else?" I ask, curious what other absurdities he'd seen.

"One of the places I used to work had this large lobby, tons of people coming in and out at all hours. Reports of a disturbance came in, and we went to go handle it. There was a man sitting on a wingback lobby chair watching porn on his phone. The volume was loud enough I could hear the moans about ten feet away. His hand was down his pants as he jerked off in front of everyone."

"Gross! What the hell?" I shake my head. "I guess he couldn't wait for his room?"

"Nope. I nearly knocked him out though. There were families nearby with their kids. Oh, I have a better one." Robert smiles brightly, and I wave him on to continue. "Sometimes I work security for the clubs. Those who pay good money or know someone"—he rolls his eyes at the latter—"can reserve VIP areas that are somewhat secluded. We are still responsible for doing rounds and making sure there are no problems. They pay enough that the managers instruct us to look the other way if it looks like consensual sex. Well, on one of these occasions, I came across this threesome. The man was naked, lying on his back while a woman rode him like a bull. Seriously, her arm was in the air, waving around." Robert pauses as laughter bursts from my lips. "While she went for her joyride, another woman rode the man's face. Nothing too shocking, and I stood watching, completely lost in the live porn in front of me."

"So what happened then?" I ask, realizing there has to be a turn in the events.

"After a little while, the woman at his mouth comes and scoots down, so she's squatting over his chest."

"Oh, no!"

He nods. "She proceeds to piss all over the man, giving him one hell of a golden shower, to which the cowgirl and man come."

I cringe, trying to envision anything but what he'd just described. "Oh, God... I don't know if I can scrub my brain from that."

"You're telling me. I walked out after that. Couldn't

touch my wife for a week afterward."

I shake my body, hoping to get rid of the image, but nothing works. "You better tell me something to make this go away!"

He chuckles, and I glare at him. "Well, all this talk about people and their sexual deviances has me wondering what yours is…"

My mouth forms an O. The conversation has taken a turn I didn't expect. "Umm… I don't have any?"

"You don't sound too sure. How about I tell you mine?" he says, his voice husky and low as he leans closer to me. "I'd love to have you watch me shower, if not in person then via video chat."

I lift my drink hoping to soothe my suddenly dry throat, but it's empty. Robert sits back. He looks relaxed and comfortable. I can't help but think he's led me here on purpose through his stories.

"Oh—" I mutter, hating how stupid I sound. My phone on the table vibrates, and I look down and see "Momma Bear calling." "I'm sorry. I need to take this," I tell him, and disappointment flashes before he nods.

"Hello… Mom?" I manage to say.

"How's it going with the dad, *darling*?" Val asks, emphasizing the endearment.

"Oh, no. That's not good," I tell her, celebrating her impeccable timing. "Yeah, I'll be on my way."

"You owe me," she tells me and hangs up.

"Is everything okay?" Robert asks.

I manage my best worried look as I gather my things. "I'm so sorry, Robert. My dad fell, and my mom needs my help."

He nods slowly. "Want me to walk you out?"

"No, I'll be fine. Thank you for tonight." I swivel on my heels and hurry out of the café. As I walk toward my car, I notice a shadow against it and freeze.

"Where's my thanks?" Val asks as she leans against the hood.

With a quick peek over my shoulder, I make sure Robert hasn't followed me out. "I was wondering how you knew to call."

"I got bored and decided to take an Uber to spy on you," she says with an unapologetic shrug.

"Stalker." I shake my head and unlock the doors. "What do I owe you?" I ask and turn the engine over.

"A sundae—the works. While I eat it, you can tell me what was wrong with him."

"That I can do. Probably for the best since I didn't have the slightest chemistry with him," I confess.

"He wasn't bad looking."

"No, he wasn't."

CHAPTER 7

"Coffee. I need coffee," I mutter to myself as I go through the cabinets in the breakroom. I stayed up way too damn late reading a book, and now here I am at work with a full day ahead of me. Not that I would have done anything differently. The story was too good to put down. It also helped drive away the occasional imagery of golden showers. I will never forgive Robert for putting those in my head.

I slam cabinets open and shut until I find my favorite mug. It isn't really mine, but I love using it. It is shaped into a large pumpkin and has faded to a dull orange. The microwave dings with my heated milk, and in minutes, the creamy goodness is at my mouth. I close my eyes and blow on the liquid before savoring the first hot sip. It is the best of them all.

"Wow, now that's what I call ecstasy!"

My eyes pop open to Mario's amused and yet darkened eyes. He recently cut his hair, and there isn't a five-o'clock shadow to be seen. Sex on a stick, that's what this man is. Too fucking bad he's already taken.

"Rough night?" he asks after I stare dumbly at him.

"Um—" Before I can finish, my phone vibrates on the counter and draws his attention away. I grab it and swipe up. Mario leans forward, close enough I can smell his aftershave, and I forget what I'm doing.

"Guess you left him wanting more," he mumbles and walks away without making himself a coffee. I follow him across the room with my eyes, confused at his abrupt departure.

The screen begins to darken, so I swipe up again. "Fucking hell!" I snap at the image of a very naked Robert in the shower. My eyes dart from the screen to the direction Mario went and back to the naked man on my screen.

It's been days since we met up at the café, and Robert hasn't messaged me once. The man's timing is impeccable, and he read my signals all wrong. You'd think after your date runs out and never replies to your messages, you'd get the hint.

Unsure about the exchange, I turn and take a large sip of my coffee. "Damn it!" I cry out after burning my tongue.

The door to the breakroom opens, and part of me hopes Mario will step back through. Two of the women who work in acquisitions laugh and look at me. We nod our hellos, and I take it as my cue to leave, burnt tongue and all.

Downstairs, I'm relieved when I find the office locked. Jerry is out, and I can enjoy a few minutes to myself. I grab my phone to close out the text that sent Mario scurrying and open the dating app.

Between sips, I scroll through the options. The man Val picked comes up, and I study his image. He's good looking with sandy-blond hair and light-brown eyes. I can imagine him in a frat. His profile mentions he has no kids, and he graduated a year earlier. He likes to go to the movies and see some of the shows that come through town.

I can see why Val picked him for me. He's not a bad choice at all. "Am I ready to do this again?" I ask myself before clicking on the envelope under his name.

Izzy_Rae: Hi! I came across your profile and was wondering if you'd like to meet for drinks.

After setting the phone down on the desk, I curl my legs under me in the computer chair. I enjoy the little bit of my now-warm coffee and try to let it all go. Maybe strictly using the dating app isn't for me. Maybe going back to in-person attraction is the way to go. After all, we've been doing it for thousands of years. *Maybe*, my mom could set me up in a prearranged marriage, dowry and all.

Now I'm being dramatic.

A noise at the counter has my eyes popping open. Jerry shakes his head at me. "Sleeping on the job?"

I smile. "Nope, resting my eyes."

***

"I'm getting a cat," I announce as I enter the kitchen in our apartment. Val is at the stove cooking and glances at me.

"Hello, sunshine. Please throw me a bone here. I thought I heard you just say you were getting a cat?"

I lean against the counter and stare at the hot dogs in the skillet. "You heard correctly. Maybe I'll go down to the humane society today. I wonder if they will have an all-black one like the one from *Hocus Pocus*."

"Yeah… no," she tells me and rolls the dogs onto a different side.

"What do you mean, no? The lease says nothing

about no animals. I can go to the office and tell them and pay the pet fee."

"No, you aren't getting a cat. Why the hell do you want a cat anyway? Do you even *like* cats?" Val asks, the spatula waving around as she emphasizes her words.

"Who doesn't like cats?"

"People who are deathly allergic to them?" she tells me.

"You're allergic to cats?"

"No—"

"Then I don't see the problem. Would you like to go with me? You can help me pick one out!"

Val shuts off the stove and grabs my arm. "Izzy... What is this about? I know it's not about cats, or dogs for that matter. Talk to me, honey."

Looking past her, I sigh. "A cat will love me and not leave me."

She laughs, and I narrow my eyes. "Cats escape all the time, and there is no guarantee they will love you. A dog will love you because dogs don't care who you are as long as you feed them and let them out. Cats? They are picky as hell." Val pulls me in and hugs me. "Girl, you can't start dating around after not doing it and expect to meet the perfect guy. It takes time, and look at me. I'm single too. Lots of people are single and struggling to find someone."

I nod and shut my teary eyes. "I'm frustrated and tired of how awful these guys are."

"Well, Mr. Slobber was only awful at kissing." She giggles.

Pulling back from her, I lean my elbows on the counter and stare at the chipped nail polish on my toes. "Yeah, I know, but I also refuse to settle."

"Then don't. You should never settle, honey."

My phone dings before I can say anything. There's a

notification on the app.

Zeke_702: Hi, I'd like to meet. How does 7 p.m. work at Enzo's?

"Who is it?" Val asks.

I reply back, letting him know the time and place work and smile. "The guy *you* picked. I asked him yesterday if he wanted to meet for drinks."

"And he's replying back now?" Val asks, annoyed at the delayed response.

I shrug. "Maybe he didn't see it until today."

"Maybe. Hey, you have no reason to settle, okay? You are hot, sweet, kind, funny, and overall an awesome person. If I didn't like dick so much, I'd hit on you."

I laugh as I shake my head. "Thanks, Val. Looks like I need to see what I'm going to wear for tonight. We will see how much better you do at picking them than me." I roll my eyes and leave the kitchen.

The date isn't for another six hours, but excitement and nerves roll through me. It's obvious I don't have good luck with men. This could go a variety of ways, and I plan on enjoying myself regardless.

"Either more comes out of it, or I'll learn something from the experience," I tell myself and pull open my closet door. Enzo's is a popular watering hole in town. It's a laid-back joint, and they like to bring in local acts. If tonight bombs, I can enjoy some good music at the least.

***

The crowd at Enzo's is thin as I make my way inside. After a quick scan, I don't see Zeke and head straight for the bar. Tonight's bartender is a girl my age. Her long wavy locks are pulled into a high ponytail, allowing her breasts to be the center of attention.

"What can I get you?" she asks with a quick smile.

My eyes move to the row of beers on tap. "I'll take the wheat beer."

Without a word, she grabs a glass and tilts it under the tap. I look around and spot an empty table a perfect distance from the stage. My phone vibrates in my hand, and I check to see if it's Zeke.

"It'll be five fifty," she tells me, and I look up after pressing on the message. "That's one hell of a text." Her brows raise with amusement before she moves down the bar, leaving my beer in front of me.

When I glance down, I'm not sure if I should laugh or run out for a restraining order. The image is of a naked and wet Robert in the shower. I'm starting to think his kink is exhibitionism. I press delete and see I have no unopened texts. After I pay for my beer, I move toward the table before it's snatched up. In the little time I spent at the bar, another twenty or so people have come in.

"Izzy?" a man asks from behind me.

I turn in my seat and smile. "Zeke?"

He stretches his hand toward me, and I put mine in it. "Nice to meet you! I see you've already gotten a drink." Zeke releases my hand. "Would you like anything else while I go grab mine?"

I smile at his manners. "I just got it, so I'm good. Hurry before the bar gets two people deep," I tell him and nod toward the people gathering.

Zeke walks away, and I take the opportunity to check him out. His body reminds me of a fit swimmer. His jeans sit nicely at his waist, hug his butt to show it off, and loosen at his legs. His collared shirt fits him well, and I'm relieved it's not popped up. Overall, he's groomed and prepared for a casual date, which makes me glad I paired a nice blouse with my skinny jeans and clutch.

He sits across from me and smiles. "I'm glad you reached out."

His smile is charming and sincere, which eases some of my nerves floating around. "Thanks for messaging me back. Do you come here often?"

Zeke looks around. "I've been a few times. I like the environment. I figured when you mentioned drinks, it would be a good spot for a first date."

"You did great." I wink, flirting with his easy demeanor.

"Which beer is that?" he asks, pointing with his own.

"The wheat. Yours?"

"Miller," he tells me, and I cringe. "What's wrong with Miller?"

"Nothing if you like flavored water," I tease.

He laughs, and it's a nice sound. "All right, I see how it is. Have you heard this band before?" he asks as the band introduces themselves.

"No, tonight will be my first time. You?"

Zeke nods. "My buddy is the drummer."

"Ah... I see you choosing Enzo's wasn't strictly for the environment?" I raise my brow and watch him shuffle in his seat.

"Ugh, well—"

I laugh and touch his hand. "I'm only messing with you." I return my hand to my lap and ask, "What kind of music are you into?"

The conversation moves along easily between us, and I relax. We tease each other and laugh, and I'm pleasantly surprised by this first date. Zeke doesn't push me in any way and hasn't exhibited or shared any behaviors that are a hard no for me.

My mind flits to Robert and his pictures, poor Johnny who can't kiss, and Brad the Chump who ditched me with the exorbitant bill. *Ugh*, I inwardly groan. I also can't forget Tristan who wanted to screw me after only a few hours of nice conversation.

I peek at Zeke whose head is bobbing to the beat. He catches me and smiles before returning his attention to the song. Maybe the tide is changing for me?

***

Zeke offers to walk me to my car. Maintaining a safe distance, he never attempts to hold my hand or even wrap his arm around me. I don't know if I should applaud him or worry after my last rounds of dates.

Looking up toward the dark sky, I sigh. "I love that we can see so many stars out here."

Zeke smiles and gazes at the stars above. "They are beautiful. I love that we have the city feel and then within fifteen, twenty minutes, we have the country feel."

"Yes! It's the best. I'm sorry I couldn't stay longer," I say when we reach my car.

He puts his hands in his pockets and shakes his head. "Don't be. Maybe we can meet up a different night?"

My face pulls back tightly with a grin. "I'd like that. Tonight was a lot of fun. It was exactly what I needed."

"Glad to hear that." Zeke leans forward and surprises me with a kiss to the cheek. "Good night, Izzy." He opens my door and waits until I'm in before shutting it. Once I turn the car on, he waves and walks back toward Enzo's.

It takes me a second to put my car in drive as I process his sweet kiss to the cheek. The romance behind it makes butterflies erupt in my stomach. Giddy with finally having a good date, I point the car toward home, excited to share my night with Val.

I shouldn't compare the men to each other, but it was silly to think I wouldn't. The conversation between Zeke and I flowed most of the night. The quiet stretches were comfortable with neither of us forcing it. He'd touched my hand a few times, soft and sweet but never pushing for more. I'll admit I'd been hoping for a good-night kiss on my lips, but the one on my cheek affected me even more.

At home, Val and I sit on the couch, oh-ing and aw-ing over my date. She wasn't willing to let go of the small detail that she was the one who picked Zeke from the selection of men. When my phone dings, we find a message from him. She bows with an exaggerated flourish and disappears to her room.

Zeke_702: I had a great time tonight.

Izzy_Rae: So did I. Great choice with going to Enzo's. Your friends sound great.

Zeke_702: Would you be interested in seeing a movie? Dinner and a movie to be precise?

Izzy_Rae: I like food, and I like movies... ha ha ha

We decide on a movie, and he tells me to choose the dinner location. Insists, really. I can't stop the smile even if I tried. Zeke's a burst of fresh air in my dating life. Part of me doesn't want to focus on it in case it blows up in my face. The other part keeps telling me to shut up and enjoy it.

I go to bed with a smile and a soundtrack of our first date.

CHAPTER 8

Classes went without a hitch this week. My stress is low, and I'm happy. The only thing I can think about is my upcoming date with Zeke. Jerry mentioned my peppiness, but I simply shrugged and put in my hours.

After the mess with Brad and the expensive Italian restaurant, I decided on a nice pub near the theater. I was surprised when Zeke told me he'd never been there.

"Where to tonight?" Val asks from my doorway.

"Nexus Pub, and after, we're going to see the latest Marvel movie," I tell her as I button my jeans.

"You're wearing *that*?" she asks, and I look from my skinny jeans to the loose blouse laid out on the bed.

"Yeah, why?" I ask and bite my lip.

Her hands go up in defense. "Nothing! I guess I thought you'd wear a dress or skirt ensemble. I like that shirt on you."

"You sure?" I slip the shirt over my head and turn toward the mirror. "Now you have me second-guessing myself!"

"Izzy! Ignore me. You look great!"

I grab my wedges from the closet and finish the look.

Once I feel pretty and comfortable, I turn to Val and roll my eyes. "You're a bitch for worrying me."

Val laughs. "I'm sorry, honey. I didn't mean to. Do you want me to call and pretend to be your mom tonight?"

"No. I didn't get any weird vibes from him last time."

I give her the theater and pub names, so she knows where I'll be, and head out. The thirty-minute drive is into a nicer part of town, but I don't drop my guard. I've seen enough shit pop up on the news to remind me no amount of money stops crime.

After parking in the casino's garage, I walk to the pub where I find Zeke waiting outside for me. He smiles as I approach and kisses my cheek when I get there.

"Is it busy?" I ask, nodding toward the hostess.

"No. We have a table, but I wanted to watch you walk up." His eyes don't meet mine with his confession. It's sweet, and I admit, I like it a lot.

"Well, I'm here." I wink after spinning in front of him.

Zeke chuckles and offers me his arm. "Yes, you are, and you look beautiful if I do say so myself."

"Thank you, you look handsome yourself," I tell him, and it's not a lie. He's wearing another pair of dark-wash jeans paired with a nice button-down dark-colored shirt. It's simple and yet perfect for our date.

He helps me into my seat before sitting across from me. "How was your day?"

I smile and tell him. We talk each day via the app, but we haven't shared our numbers. It's silly since by now when I was talking to Johnny, his dirty talk had me all hot and bothered.

Maybe I'm only trying to not repeat the same mistakes?

"I'm so excited to see the movie and that you don't think I'm acting like a kid for seeing it," he confesses.

"Oh, no! I love these movies! My roommate Val will see a lot with me, but these aren't one. I usually end up seeing the comic movies by myself."

"A beautiful woman by herself at the theater? What a shame!" His eyes sparkle with his charming words.

I shrug. "Sometimes it's nice to go by myself. I can see whatever I want and not worry about making the other person happy."

"That's very true. I wish I would have thought about that years ago."

Dinner with Zeke goes exceptionally well. I'm stuffed and have a slight buzz from the two beers I enjoyed. I'm a fucking light weight, I know. Warmth brushes my fingers as we walk to the theater, and I meet his eyes.

His fingers link with mine, and the simple touch makes me smile. My attraction for Zeke isn't instantaneous, but that doesn't matter to me. I'm sure as hell enjoying the slow burn. The time I'm spending with him is allowing me to get to know him. Butterflies have spread their wings at the new experience.

But will they still be here in a few months? I shove the internal voice aside, wishing I could punch her in the face.

Zeke buys our tickets, and I laugh when he asks if I want popcorn. I'm stuffed as a turkey, and the idea of eating more makes me sick. I do, however, tell him I'd love another beer.

We carry our beers to the theater and find the perfect seats in the middle. I look at him, and he's as giddy as a child. It's so cute; I can't help but smile. I put my hand on my thigh and wonder if he will grab it during the movie. I'm acting like a damn teenage girl.

Somehow, I manage to force aside my immature reactions to this man. My phone vibrates in my purse, and I shoot Val a quick text reassuring her everything is okay. As the lights start to dim, a familiar man walks in with a pretty woman.

I can't help but notice the couple as they pick the seats in front of us. My eyes peek down at them throughout the entire movie. They steal kisses and cuddle together and are unlike so many couples I've seen. They seem genuinely happy.

When the lights come on, Zeke gushes about the movie. I nod as I notice the rock on the woman's hand. Robert meets my eyes, and they round before he pretends he doesn't know me. He's a reminder that not all are who they seem to be.

I peek up at Zeke and his childlike smile as we walk out of the theater with our trash in tow. After he relieves his hands of his half-filled bag of popcorn and drink, he grabs my hand in his.

He squeezes my hand. "Do you want to walk around, or do you need to head home?"

"I'd love to walk around, but I have an assignment I need to work on." I give him a playful pout, and he nods.

"I'll walk you to your car then," Zeke says, and we make our way toward the elevators. "Tonight was fun."

"It was!"

"Okay, since we didn't get a chance to chat during the movie, how about a quick round of twenty questions?"

I smile. "Sure, why not. Do I get to go first?" When he nods, I ask, "What country is on your bucket list?"

"Greece. When you aren't studying, working, or going out with me…" He winks, and I shake my head at him. "What do you like to do?"

"I'm either reading or watching Netflix. What's your

favorite holiday?" I ask as my car appears ahead.

"Easy, Easter. What—"

"What? Easter? Really? Why?"

"Rapid-fire questions?" He chuckles. "I love chocolate. Easter always has chocolate."

I laugh. "So does Valentine's day... Halloween... Hell, even Christmas has those advent calendars with chocolate."

He shrugs. "I don't know. I just do. Okay, last question. Can I kiss you?" he asks as he turns me.

His hands lightly hold my hips, but our bodies don't touch. The butterflies in my stomach flutter with excitement. I nod, and he steps closer to me. My heart speeds as his lips lower to mine. They're soft and warm against my mouth. Zeke cups my cheek as we exchange a sweet, tender kiss.

Tilting my head, I silently invite him to deepen the kiss. When it doesn't turn for the worse, I smile against his lips. It's a great first kiss, one I will remember fondly. Zeke pulls back, and his face is soft as his eyes crinkle with a smile. After a moment of watching me, he presses a chaste kiss against my lips and steps back.

"Good night, Izzy," he whispers, his eyes flicking down to my mouth.

"Night, Zeke. I had a really nice time."

***

"So?" Val asks from the couch as I let myself in.

"What are you watching?" I ask, kicking off my shoes.

"Fifty Shades. Now you, how'd it go?"

I drop on the couch next to her. "It was great. We even kissed." I grin.

Val faces me. "Well, it doesn't look like he tried drowning you to death. I assume it was good?"

I nod. "Yup, a great first kiss by all accounts. Why do you watch this movie so much?"

"Grey is hot."

"You realize you'd go running the other way with a real Dom, right? This is still all fiction?" I ask her.

She sighs. "Yeah, I know. Let me enjoy this fantasy, all right?"

I throw my hands in the air. "Have at it. Oh, you won't believe who I saw."

"Who?"

"Robert, the shower guy."

"Nuh-uh! Was he by himself?" she asks, her eyes wide.

I laugh dryly. "Nope. I think she's his wife or maybe someone else's wife. There was a rock on her finger. They were all lovey-dovey."

"Bastard," she says with a shake of her head.

I nod as I stand. "Enjoy your movie. I have homework, and I open tomorrow."

***

I stare at the trash can symbol a moment before touching it with my thumb. I've been seeing Zeke for a few weeks now, and things are moving along nicely. We've moved on to texting via our phones rather than the messenger. There really isn't a need for me to have Lucky in Love on my phone.

Setting it aside, I smile and notice the time. I have a few minutes left until I can grab food before my night class. Jerry's gone for the day, and the next person won't come in for another thirty minutes.

The paper rounds are done, and the machines will hold up until they arrive. A few hours passed since I checked the supplies on the table. Not many students have come in, but I look them over anyway.

Lost in the mindless job, I nearly throw the largest of the staplers when someone grabs my hips. Turning quickly, I find Zeke's large smile and twinkling eyes staring down at me.

"Oh my God! You scared the shit out of me!" I snap.

He shrugs. "Well, I couldn't help touching you." Zeke lowers his mouth to mine, and my hands move up his body to lock behind his neck.

"Mmm… hi," I mutter when he pulls back. I hear voices as students pass the door, reminding me I am still in the office. I step back with a smile. "What are you doing here?"

Zeke reaches to the side, and I spot the single red rose he placed on the counter. "I came to see you. I brought you this, and I hoped I could take you to eat before you rushed off to class."

After the series of men before him, Zeke is a godsend. This simple action makes me resent my class, and I wish I could spend my evening with him instead.

"That's really sweet! Thank you!" I kiss him quickly and bring the rose to my nose. "Well, let me grab my things, and we can head out."

Once the lights are off, I lock the door and make sure the sign says when someone will be back. Zeke grabs my hand in his as we walk away. As per usual, I turn toward Circulation. "I need to make a quick stop."

Dark eyes meet mine before flicking to Zeke. I force myself to face the supervisor on duty and not the brooding man who doesn't look happy to see me. "Hey! I'm out for the night, but Kristina comes in in about thirty minutes. The machines are all set for now."

Robin looks from me to Zeke and smiles. "Thanks, Izzy!"

"No problem." I glance one last time at Mario, whose jaw muscle is twitching, before I pull Zeke toward the door.

Outside, Zeke nods toward the building. "Who was the guy?"

"Huh?" I ask, playing dumb. What am I supposed to say? He's a hot guy in the building who I bump into literally and figuratively?

"The guy shooting daggers at me. Is he an ex or someone you shot down?"

"That's Mario. Not an ex, no shooting down either. We only work together in the building. What do you want to eat?" I ask, hoping to change the topic.

Zeke chuckles. "That man looked at me like I stole his favorite toy."

"What?" I ask. I really am dumbfounded. Mario has never looked at me in any *specific* kind of way. I wanted him to, but what is the point now? He has a girlfriend, and I'm with Zeke.

"Izzy, you're hot. Any guy would be stupid not to think so." Zeke points backward with his thumb. "That guy? He's not stupid. He thinks so too."

I shrug. "Well..." I raise the rose to my nose and smell. "It doesn't matter now, does it? I'm seeing a really sweet man who brings me roses and walks me to dinner before class."

Zeke wraps his arm around my shoulder and pulls me in. "I'm glad you think so." He kisses my temple, and we decide to eat at the sub place on campus.

CHaPTer 9

"What are you doing?" Val asks as I shove her toward the door after tossing her purse at her.

"*We* are going shopping. You are going to help me pick out some new bra-and-panty sets."

"Wh—Oh my God! Are you going to sleep with him?" She squeals.

I look around, hoping none of the neighbors heard her. Who am I kidding? Zeke probably heard her big mouth. "Why are you so damn loud?"

"You are!"

I shake my head at her excitement. "You need to make yourself scarce tonight," I tell her at the bottom of the stairs.

"How long have you two been seeing each other now?" she asks as we walk toward my car.

"Long enough to feel comfortable?"

Val laughs. "Long enough to stop your dry spell is more like it. Good for you!" She clears her throat and smiles. "So, should I mention this guy you are comfortable with is the one I picked out?"

I unlock the car and flip her off before getting in.

"Shut up, will you?"

Her only response is to laugh louder at me.

Thankfully, she drops the subject on the drive to the mall. We don't get a lot of time to hang out anymore now that I've been seeing Zeke a little more frequently. She also met a guy but has postponed their first date.

"So why don't you meet up with the coffee barista tonight?"

She sighs and looks out the window. "I don't know about that."

"Val, honey. Not every guy is like your ex. You can't knock them all down. I thought you said this guy was cute and really sweet?"

"He is. It's just hard," she whispers. The normally confident woman is replaced by the shattered pieces of heartbreak.

"I know it is. Sometimes it doesn't feel worth the trouble. Remember this: the longer you avoid dating again, the longer you let that asshole win. He's not in your life, and yet he is still controlling your happiness. Don't let him have that," I whisper and decide I've said enough on the subject.

When we arrive at the mall, my stomach groans loudly, and we burst into laughter. "It seems we need to feed you first," Val says, her earlier sorrow only a memory.

I put a hand to my stomach. "No kidding!"

We enter the mall and head straight for the food court. We join the early crowd as they grab their bite of food. Our conversation is always easy and open. I've known Val for a couple years, but it's as if we've known each other since childhood. I guess sometimes it doesn't matter how long you've known a person. That connection isn't something you can fake.

"Ready to make him come on the spot?" Val teases.

"Wait, no, that would be bad. Oh, God, what if he's a two-second man?"

My nerves were already all over the place since I made the decision to move on to the next step. "Val, shut up. You're going to make me puke. I'm already nervous as it is."

She nods. "You're right. Plus, you've already had all the bad luck you can get. Everything should go great with Zeke."

I slap her arm. "Why on earth would you go and say that? Fucking jinxing me?" My heart speeds up at all the awful things that could go wrong.

"It's not like you're going to pull a muscle. Everything will be fine. You could use some great sex to calm the hell down." Val grabs my arm and leads me to the lingerie store. She yammers on about what styles I should go with when all I can think of is if I should wait longer.

My phone vibrates, and I find an unread text from Zeke as if he knows I'm freaking out.

Zeke: Are we still on for tonight? You don't need to cook for me. I can take you out somewhere.

Izzy: I want to cook for you. We can have a nice night in, unless of course you'd rather go out?

Zeke: I'm not going to turn away a home-cooked meal. If I'm hanging out with you, I'll be happy.

Izzy: Great, I'll see you at six.

I can't help but smile as I read the texts. My nerves calm some, and I find Val staring at me while we stand in front of crotchless panties.

"You're smiling, so I'm guessing it's Zeke?"

"Yeah. He wanted to confirm our plans for tonight."

Val grabs the underwear. "Good. Now what do you think about these?"

"Nope," I say, shaking my head back and forth. "Not

going to happen."

She sighs. "You're no fun."

"Why don't you meet the coffee guy and wear those for him?" I tell her, raising my brows suggestively. Val puts them back immediately before wrapping her fingers around my wrist and yanking.

I laugh at her reaction. "Oh, so they were good enough for me but not for you?"

"Shut up!"

Wandering around the store for fifteen minutes, I realize all the things I don't want to wear. In one corner, I finally find sets that are more me. I grab a set of lacy undergarments that are teal, violet, and black. The bra has no wire, and after trying it on, I confirm my nipples will show in a sexy tease. The thongs are like my everyday ones but in lace.

On my way to the cashier, I spot a nightie that causes my cheeks to flush. The delicate material slips between my fingers, and I can't help but sigh. I imagine the soft satin against my naked skin, but I can't bring myself to grab my size.

"Hot damn that is sexy," Val mutters from my side.

"Isn't it beautiful..."

"You have to get it," she says and begins looking at the sizes. "Here!"

"I don't think I can wear that," I whisper. It's one thing to start making out and have it turn into more. I've never worn a nightie solely to lure a man into bed. The idea of starting now, with Zeke, makes my palms damp.

"Buy it. You can either wear it this time or another. This way, you have something more *comfortable* to slip into. This material is divine. I'm almost tempted to get one for myself, only I know it will go unused. At least you have a chance in hell of using it in the next few months if not tonight." Val's words are soft and encouraging.

Her teasing tone is gone as we continue staring at the beautiful nightie. It screams romance and love, unlike the over-the-top crotchless underwear we are too shy to wear. Before I change my mind, I grab the outstretched hanger and rush to the cashier. Each piece is delicately wrapped and put in a bag away from prying eyes.

"You're going to knock him dead," Val tells me and winks.

"As long as I don't send him running out the door, I'll count it as a win."

CHAPTER 10

Once we return from the mall, Val helps me clean the apartment and work on dinner. After I left enough time to shower, I pluck and shave every unwanted hair, scrub my skin with an exfoliant, and lather my body in a nice lotion that claims to slow the aging process. It was probably complete bull, but it didn't hurt to try.

My head is upside down as I blow-dry my hair when Val's legs appear. I shut off the dryer and brush my damp hair. "What's up?"

"I'm heading out now and the casserole is out of the oven. I'll be at the café for a while and then I'll catch a late show. Make sure you dirty kids are behind closed doors by the time I return. I don't need a visual of all the sex I'm not having."

I laugh at Val and hug her before hurrying to finish getting ready. If I'm not careful, I'll be answering the door in nothing but a towel, effectively speeding up the process to what I hope will be a hot romp between the sheets.

After more work than I like, I'm ready. To the outsider, I would look nice and yet relaxed as if I hadn't put in as much work into the process as I actually did.

The food will be our appetizer before the main course. And by main course, I'm hoping for hot, sweaty sex that will leave me limp as a noodle. My poor body has been sorely neglected, and it's ready for someone to take advantage of it.

The doorbell rings, and I glance around the room. Everything looks fine, not like I left cheesy candles covering the surfaces. The only one lit is centered on the coffee table to help the room smell nice. Not that I expect a man to notice that sort of thing. It did, however, help me relax.

Knock. Knock. Knock.

"Crap," I mutter, realizing I've fallen into my thoughts while he waits outside. Using the peephole, I see Zeke and smile before opening the door. "Hi!"

He looks me over with appreciation. "You look beautiful." Zeke kisses me softly, and I move so he can enter the apartment.

A bouquet of seasonal flowers appears from behind his back, and I bring them to my nose. "Thank you, these are pretty."

"You're welcome. Nice place you've got."

"Thanks, it's just us tonight. My roommate, Val, has plans and won't be home until late. I hope you're hungry." I rush the last part, hoping I don't sound too obvious about how I expect our night to go.

His eyes move down my body, and unmistakable desire shines from them. "Starving."

I pour us each a glass of wine with dinner. No, it's not what's left over from my date with Brad the Asshole Chump. Val bought me a special bottle just for tonight. She's as excited as I am for me to finally get some.

Dinner goes smoothly, and his compliments keep a constant blush across my cheeks. I've always done well in the kitchen, but it's never been my passion. Since men can be assholes, it's one fact I kept off the dating app. Last thing I want is a man who wants to date me because I can do more than toast bread.

We clean up and move to the living room. I head toward the couch and pick up the remote as I sit. "I didn't know what you would like to watch, so I figured we could rent something or search Netflix."

"Whatever you want to watch," Zeke says and pulls me into his side. His warmth relaxes me, and I finally settle on a movie I've watched a million times. I lay my hand on his thigh and place my head comfortably against him.

I'm not sure how much time has passed, but I know his fingertips caressing the side of my arm is driving me crazy. I can't help wondering what he's packing and how he'll fill me. When Zeke doesn't make the first move, I excuse myself and pass the bathroom.

Staring into my dresser drawer at the lacy number, I debate whether to pull it out. Do I want to go there? Should I be this blunt? Will it be a turn off for him? Has a guy ever been turned off by a woman who wants to be taken to bed?

Finally, I shake my head free of the crazy thoughts. Instead of donning the sexy little nightie, I return to the living room and straddle his lap without a word. Zeke's eyes round a moment before darkening with interest. I lower my mouth to his, and his hands cup my hips, massaging the flesh before digging his fingertips into me.

I taste the wine we drank as our kiss deepens. As our hands roam about, he hardens under me. His fingers slip under my shirt and find my bare belly. His warm touch grazes and teases my skin. God, it's been too long since I've had sex!

His tongue caresses mine, and I moan against his

mouth. The kiss is sweet and tempting and *great!* Then again, any kiss that doesn't involve slobber is a winner. The bar has been set rather low after Johnny. Forcing my mind to focus, I run my fingers through his hair, and his hands slide up and down my sides.

I don't care at this point if he thinks I'm too forward. Zeke needs to know without a doubt where I want him next. I pull back and grab the hem of my shirt. With years of experience, it's over my head and tossed aside in a single moment.

His eyes drop to my breasts, and I know what he sees. My pink nipples, hard from arousal, through the thin lace.

Zeke's answering groan makes me grin. Encouraged by his reaction, I reach behind me. With a flick, the cups loosen, and the straps begin to slip. Zeke slides off my bra, and I give him a second, letting him enjoy the view and hoping I don't have to draw arrows for what I want.

"God, you have great tits!" he mutters as one finger runs along the tops of my breasts. He cups them both, and my head rolls to the side. His thumbs graze the tight buds before he plucks and tweaks them. The touch sends bolts of electricity down between my legs.

I feel his eyes on my face and meet them. He squeezes a little more, and they flutter closed as a moan slips free. My hips rotate with wanton need at the pleasure. He pulls one taut nipple into his mouth, and I press harder against his thickness, frustration building at the cumbersome jeans separating us.

Zeke teases one breast and then the other before he lays me down on the cushion seats. He leaves a trail of kisses down my stomach while his fingers fumble with my jeans. When he stills, I meet his eyes. I bite my lip and lift my hips in silent reply. Zeke watches me closely as he pulls them down my legs.

He looks from my lacy underwear to the discarded bra and smiles. "Matching set? Izzy, did you ask me over to have your way with me?"

I giggle even as my cheeks warm. "Is it working?"

His eyes rake over my nearly nude body. I mean, the lacy underwear isn't exactly hiding what is under them. "Oh, yeah."

The pure lust shining from his eyes and the tone of his words push away any doubt. "Good. For a second, I thought you were complaining," I tell him and wink.

Hooking the band of my underwear with his fingers, he pulls them down slowly. "*Fuuuck* no. I'm not complaining at all."

Raising each leg, I slip them from my underwear. Zeke tosses the scrap of fabric aside and sits on his heels. Two fingers run over me, teasing my flesh. My breaths come in short pants as the need to be filled coils tighter in my belly. I gasp when his fingers push into me, curling and hitting my magical spot. His thumb puts pressure on my clit, making little circles that send my nerves into overdrive.

Zeke's mouth covers my nipple, and I hold his head in place. My body is winding tighter with each stroke of his tongue and the magic his fingers cast. It won't take long for my body to fall apart.

I check another block for Zeke. He knows how to use his hands. Secretly, I plead with him for more, but I want to see what else he has in his bag of tricks.

As the thought forms in my mind, I release his head, and he scatters kisses down my belly. When his warm, wet tongue replaces his thumb, I buck. Looking down with surprise, I find him watching me. His fingers pick up their speed, and he sucks my clit into his mouth. He flicks his tongue over it, and in moments, my back is arching off the couch as spots burst behind my eyelids.

Zeke tongues me gently. Each time it runs along the sensitive bud, my legs twitch. All movement stops, and I look down through the fog of my climax. He brings his fingers to his mouth, wrapping his lips tightly around them and sucking me off his skin.

"So sweet," he mutters.

I lift to my elbows, but before I can reach out to work his jeans, Zeke drives his tongue into me. Without any grace, I fall back onto the couch and let out a loud moan. I relax and take the pleasure he's intent on giving me, letting my worries slip free with each swipe of his talented tongue.

There is no time. No place to be. No thoughts to be had. I'm enjoying this man's mouth between my legs with full abandon. Zeke replaces his mouth with his fingers and draws my clit into his warm mouth. He mercilessly flicks at the bundle of nerves, and I'm lost.

"Oh! I'm coming!" I cry and grind against his hand.

The haze of my orgasm fades, and I realize he is no longer between my legs. He shucks his pants and stands next to the couch. His hand runs up and down his shaft. My eyes take him in.

"You like my dick?" he asks, his eyes heavy-laden with desire.

I bite my lip and nod.

"Look how thick this cock is," Zeke says, releasing himself so I can see it from a few angles. "It's going to stretch that pussy of yours."

My desire dims, momentarily confused at what he's going on about. He thrusts himself into his hand and swirls his hips. I've never had a man pay this much attention to himself in the middle of foreplay and find this a little odd. I look at his thickness. Sure, it has a nice girth, maybe even the thickest I've been with, but that's not saying a whole lot either.

Zeke grabs his jeans from the ground and removes a foil packet. The sound of it ripping open pierces the fog addling my brain, and I remember where we're at. I roll off the couch and onto my feet.

"Wait, not here." I grab his wrist after he rolls on the condom.

We hurry down the hall, and I glance back when he groans. "What?"

"You have a great ass," he tells me, and I smile. Inside the room, I stop at the edge of the bed and look at him. "Get on the bed, Izzy," Zeke demands in a low voice before he shuts and locks the door.

I do as he says, lying my head on a pillow in the center. I melt into the bed in a post-orgasm state of bliss. My heart beats rapidly as he stalks toward me. Zeke has a great body, toned muscles wrapping his slender frame. He climbs onto the bed and kneels between my legs. He lowers his face to mine, and I wrap my arms around him as our kiss deepens.

Shifting his hips, he presses against my entrance. I raise my hips and relish the fullness I feel when he seats himself after a few slow pumps.

Zeke moans against my mouth. "You're so tight."

He moves against me, and the first few strokes border on uncomfortable, but once my body adjusts, there's only pleasure. After two orgasms, my sex is over sensitized. My hips meet each of his thrusts with short shallow breaths escaping my lips.

Zeke sits back on his heels and lifts my hips to his. His eyes move to our connection, and I follow the path. The erotic view has my muscles tightening around him.

"Are you okay?" he asks, his head tilted to the side.

"Yes, more than okay." The way he fills me is new and exciting. His thickness takes my breath away to be honest. This is the most stretched I've ever been. My girlie bits are happy to finally get attention from someone other than me or a vibrator.

His head tips to the side again. "You're so damn tight. I bet I'm the biggest cock you've had."

My brows draw together with confusion. I know men like to mark their territory, but his words sound weird to me. I've already allowed him between my legs. He doesn't have to talk himself up.

"Does my dick feel great inside you? I bet it does. I know being in this pussy is amazing." Another tip of his head has me wondering if he's okay.

I still, but Zeke doesn't notice. He continues to go on about his dick and how good it must be for me.

I'm totally weirded out now. What is wrong with his head?

His head moves rhythmically to the side, again and again. Oh my God, he's twitching with each thrust of his hips!

I can't help but stare as I process it all. My desire is long gone, nowhere to be seen, but he doesn't seem to notice. I'm not sure if thirty seconds have passed or five minutes since I quit being into the sex, but finally he groans.

"I'm going to come. My big dick is going to fill this condom for you."

Nope. This is just all sorts of weird. What the hell do I do?

There is only one thing I can think to do. I inwardly cringe as I tighten my muscles around him. "Oh!" My fake orgasm sounds weak, and I worry he will notice.

"Yes! Take my cock!" Zeke cries out as he pumps two more times before collapsing on me.

Lying in bed with Zeke panting in the crook of my neck, I stare at the ceiling. I'm not sure what twilight zone I entered. Everything with him had been great. It's why I was ready to take this next step. Val may think I'm being picky, but there is no way in hell I can do this again.

After a few minutes, he lifts his body and I shut my eyes, pretending to be asleep when in reality I'm freaking the hell out.

"Izzy? You fall asleep on me?" he asks, and I mumble incoherently. I rub my head into my pillow, trying to get more comfortable.

"Mmm… night… Val… coming home…"

He shuffles around my room, and I imagine he's looking for my trash can. I force my eyes to remain closed, wishing this night to be done. His warm breath caresses my cheek. "Good night. I'm sure you're all worn out. I'll see myself out."

I wait almost ten minutes after he shuts my bedroom door before I get out of bed. "What the fuck just happened?" My eyes move to the nightstand where I keep my vibrator. "Maybe I should quit dating. Nothing says you can't just stick to self-love."

I snag my phone and unlock it.

Izzy: It's safe to come home.

Val: Already? You okay?

Izzy: Fucking twilight zone.

Val: Really? I didn't see that one coming.

Izzy: Just wait until I tell you where it all went south…

Hopefully a long, hot shower can wash away Zeke from my skin and the whole bag of crazy he brought to my bed. "Shit… I'm going to have to change those sheets before I go to sleep tonight. Ugh!"

CHAPTER 11

It's been a month since that horrid mess of a sexual encounter with Zeke. I forced myself to see him one more time in a very public setting and broke it off with him. I'm not a bitch, but no, I can't repeat that event.

Seriously, all signs pointed to me having sex with him. He didn't have to talk his dick up to me; I was a sure thing. And then that tic of his! I honestly hope he finds someone who will love him for all his quirks. I'm just not her.

I haven't succumbed and downloaded the app again. There were too many weird ones on there, or maybe it's me. Maybe I attract the wrong men. Since then, I haven't dated anyone. I'm focused on studying, working, and hanging out with Val.

We went out to a bar a week ago, and this really cute guy approached our table. I loved how smitten he'd been with Val. She balked at first. Okay, I'll admit it. I kicked her under the table until she agreed to see him again. I hope she has better luck than me.

A noise draws my attention from my musings, and I find a guy watching me in between stapling his papers.

"Do you need any help?" I ask out of habit.

His smile is almost pretty. "No, I'm good… I just got distracted for a second there."

When he winks, I read between the lines and can't help it when my cheeks warm. It really doesn't take much for me to blush. It's embarrassing how quickly it happens. I nod at him and lower my eyes to the sheet in my hands, but I can't read the words in front of me. The man in the room grabs his papers and walks to the counter.

My eyebrow raises in question, and his damn smile beams at me. "Would you be interested in getting a cup of coffee with me?"

"Umm…" I wasn't really expecting him to ask me out. I stare back at him and note the way his eyes crinkle with his smile. He's older than me by about ten years at least. "Are you a student?" I ask with a nod toward his papers.

He lifts the stack as if he forgot they were there, and that's when I see the band. "No, these are for a class I'm teaching. I'm an adjunct professor in the history department."

I point at his left hand. "You're married?" I ask the question, but he's wearing the band, so I know he is. Unless of course he's a widower who hasn't been able to move on, but there's a slim chance of that.

He smirks at me. "Yeah."

"And you just asked me out for coffee?"

"It's just coffee, not sleeping in my office," he says and shrugs.

This man is something else. I may break things off with guys because they can't kiss or they twitch during sex, but I do not—under any circumstances—do anything with a married man. I shake my head slowly because I'm stunned. "Yeah… no. How about you reserve those coffee dates for the woman you took vows with?"

His face reddens, and his eyes narrow. "Fuck you, it's your loss," he snaps before stomping away, reminding me of a toddler whose toy's been taken from him.

"Wow," I mutter and stare at the open door. I stand and walk around the counter to the doorway. When I peer out, I barely catch a glimpse of the man as he leaves the building. I shake my head as I process the scene that lasted maybe a minute.

That's how Jerry finds me. "Hey, what's up with you?"

"You won't believe this guy who was just in here," I say and tell him about the man.

Jerry shakes his head. "Some people have no morals."

"Ain't that the truth. I'm going to go do a round," I say and grab the stocked cart. We try to check the machines every hour, and they are usually fine, but occasionally I come across one that received a lot of loving in the hour.

On my way back to the office, I'm on the elevator making note of the supplies I've used when Mario steps on. He's wearing a black polo and khaki cargo shorts. His backpack is slung over his shoulder, and his hair is sticking up in spots as if he's run his hands through it a couple hundred times. He looks really good, and a little shiver of need pulses along my skin.

Girlfriend, I remind myself, and an image of the jerk from earlier pops in my head.

"Hey," I say as our eyes meet.

His smile is forced, and I can see he looks stressed out. "Hi, Izzy."

My brows knit together. "You okay?"

His phone buzzes before he can answer. I can't help

but notice he doesn't look happy at whoever's name is on the screen. He presses the side button and drops his phone back into his pocket. "I've got a test coming up, so I'm just—"

"Stressed?" I ask and give him a sympathetic smile. College is supposed to be our prime years. Anyone who's graduated tells me to enjoy the time, but shit, they must have forgotten all the studying, tests, and papers. The papers and projects always manage to weigh you down like a boulder.

Mario nods. "Yeah." His eyes pierce mine before moving to my lips. They stay there a few seconds before the bell goes off and the doors open. "Nice seeing you," he mutters and hurries out. His shoulders hunch over, the stress of the world weighing him down.

***

"Hey, girlfriend," Val calls when she enters the office.

I look up and smile. She's perky as hell for being on campus, and I can thank Mason for that. She finally took my advice and gave him her number. It's been about two weeks since they met, and for the last week she's been like this.

"Hey! You look happy," I say and push to my feet.

"Mason is so freaking sweet," she gushes.

I laugh and give her my cockiest smile. "You're welcome," I tell her in a singsong voice.

"Shut up!"

"What? I'm just glad that so far you don't have m—"

Val reaches and slams her hand over my mouth. "Don't you dare finish that statement, Unlucky Izzy!" Unlucky Izzy is the new nickname she's given me after so many failed attempts at dating. "I'm going to let go now, and you will not finish that sentence!"

I nod and she releases her hand, but not before I lick her palm.

"Eww! That's gross!"

I shrug. "Guess you shouldn't have put your hand over my mouth."

Val gives me a dirty look, and I smile.

"What brings you around here? I thought you'd forgotten where the library was?"

"My phone died during class, and I forgot my cable. Do you happen to have yours so I can borrow it?" She bats her eyes for added measure before I turn and rummage through my bag. After finding what she wants, I hand it to her. "Thank you!"

"Yeah, yeah, yeah! If you weren't texting lover boy so much, it wouldn't be dead," I say in my best mom voice.

"He's so... *different.* I'm still terrified." She whispers the latter.

I snag her hand. "I know my track record isn't helping, but not every guy out there is a douchebag. Let him show his true colors, and if he turns out to be another one, I'll be right here to help you pick up the pieces. Okay?"

Her eyes shine with unshed tears, and she gives me a small nod. "Okay."

"Where you off to now?" I ask, hoping to distract her from the fear overwhelming her.

"The coffee shop to study." She raises the cord in her hand. "Thanks again. I'll see you at home?"

"Yup."

Val leaves soon after a quick goodbye, and I return to my desk to work on a paper.

"Meeting is done," Jerry calls out to me, and I jump.

"I'm going to go do rounds."

"Okay!" I tell him and look at the time. Not a single soul had come in since Val left until Jerry startled me—an hour of uninterrupted time.

"Jinx," I whisper to myself when an older man enters the office. "Can I help you?"

He looks around, then points at the table. "Stapler. Found it, thanks."

"No problem. Let me know if you need anything else," I tell him and return to the paper staring back at me on my laptop. Only, I can't concentrate on the words. The man keeps glancing at me.

"Excuse me?" he mutters.

I force a smile. "Yes?"

"Has anyone told you that you look like that actress..." He snaps his fingers, trying to recall whomever he's thinking of. "You know, the one from the movie about the singer?"

"No, I've never been told I look like any celebrity."

"Really? You're beautiful. You should model, or if you're interested, I know this talent scout." He reaches into his pocket and produces a business card.

Not wanting to come off as rude, I stand and accept the card. "Thanks, I'll look into it."

"Yeah, I think you should. They're always looking for the next big thing, and you might just have it." He staples one last set of papers and gives me a quick wave before exiting the office.

The entire encounter leaves me unsure. My skeptical nature makes me want to chuck the card into the trash immediately, but I can't help but be curious. What would it be like to act or model professionally?

I sit and minimize the document I was working on and pull up the internet. I type in the information on the card and search everything I can think of on this "talent scout." Twenty minutes later, I haven't found a darn thing and decide to toss the card in the trash.

***

"Morning, Izzy!"

The polite greeting washes over me, and my body perks at the sound of my name rolling off Mario's lips. Sure, it's not the first time he's said my name, but today it sounds *different*. I turn and lean my hip against the counter. "Hi," I say and drink him in, a little more than I probably should.

He grabs the carafe and pours himself a cup of coffee. His dark-wash jeans hang off his hips just right. The angle lets me enjoy the way his jeans hug his ass. *Is it as firm as it looks?* He turns toward me with his mug in hand. The short-sleeve, button-up shirt he's wearing is a lighter blue and reminds me of the Caribbean. I squeeze my hands around my mug to ward off the temptation of stepping forward to see if he smells as good as he looks.

"What?" Mario asks and looks down his front. "Did I spill?"

"No, just noticing your nice shirt," I say and lift my coffee to my lips.

His eyes light up, and a dimple indents the side of his smile. "Thanks."

I should go. I haven't checked the machines this morning, and I'm sure Jerry is about to arrive. Except Mario's smile keeps me rooted to the spot. "Do you always drink it black?"

Inwardly I cringe at my words. There were a hundred different things I could ask or say, and I went with the most common small talk topics. His eyebrow raises, and I see his amusement, but he doesn't tease me.

"Yeah, black coffee, and depending on my mood is whether I add sugar to it."

I nod. "I'm not sure how you do it. I need milk in mine. Something about this caramel color is utter perfection." I take a sip as he stares at my mouth.

"It is a great color." He winks and shows me the back of his hand.

The door opens, and Jerry strides in. "Morning, I see we all need a picker-upper today."

"Yup," Mario and I mutter, and our eyes lock for a second.

He has a girlfriend. Off limits, Izabella!

"Well, I'll see you guys around. Enjoy your coffee," Mario tells us and walks toward the door. He opens it but doesn't step through, catching me checking him out. "Hey, Izzy?"

"Yeah?"

"That color suits you." Mario winks and raises his mug toward mine. Before I can ask what he means— because I'm utterly confused—he's gone. It doesn't help that my mind wandered in and out as his full lips moved.

Why did he just wink? I look from the T-shirt I'm wearing to my mug of coffee. One a dark caramel and the other blue.

Jerry leans over my mug. "What was he talking about?"

I shrug. "I'm not really sure." I leave Jerry in the breakroom and head downstairs in case there are any early birds. I take my time, the conversation with Mario weighing heavily on me. I'm not sure what he meant or what happened, and I can't seem to let it go.

My phone vibrates, drawing my attention to safer thoughts when I see Val's text.

Val: Are we still on for dinner tonight?

Izzy: Yeah, I'll have to meet you there unless you

want to wait for me?

Val: I'll wait for you.

Izzy: Do you have a second?

Val: For you, always! What's wrong? Aren't you at work?

Izzy: Yeah, just started. This strange exchange happened, and I'm not sure what it means or if it means anything.

I text Val the incident, making sure not to leave out any details. As I sit all alone in the office, I'm thankful Jerry is still out and about. One look at me and he'd ask me what is up. Knowing Jerry, he'd find Mario and ask him about it, effectively embarrassing the shit out of me. I doubt Jerry knows about Mario's girlfriend or much about the man in general, but he's a man who cuts to the chase.

My phone vibrates, and I fumble to unlock it.

Val: Mason is here, and I told him the situation.

"Damn it, Val!" I snap, even though she can't hear me.

Val: Mario's the guy we ran into who has a girlfriend, right? If so, isn't he tan? Similar color to the coffee you drink?

I hear his words again. *That color suits you.* As soon as I process the information with Val and Mason's two cents, I dismiss it.

Izzy: It is. Never mind. I must have heard him wrong.

I set the phone to silent and finish my drink. Mario is hot. He's a man you can't help but look at twice. The fact he's got a girlfriend makes him a hard no. Even now as I finish my coffee, guilt washes over me at the little bit I flirted with him. With a sigh, I stuff him into an imaginary box and push him to the side.

I remind myself I'm taking a break from all that anyway and open my laptop. Except it doesn't matter how many lies I tell myself. Mario's handsome face isn't far.

CHAPTER 12

Today is dragging.

Christmas break is coming up, which means more students are milling around as they struggle to complete papers and study for tests. The busier we are in the library, the more I need to check the machines. It's early afternoon, and I don't know how many times I've left the office to help with paper jams or to fill the paper.

Jerry and I have taken turns, but back-to-back students needing help has left us closing the office. I make sure the door is locked and head toward the bank of elevators before going left as a short cut. My feet hurt as I walk across the large floor and consider my own papers that aren't being worked on.

A strange sensation comes over me, and when I look back, I see a man I recognize, but I can't place him. Since I see a lot of the same people, I make a mental note but brush him off while I find the frustrated students trying to photocopy research material.

Within a few minutes, the students thank me, and I round the outer wall of the floor toward the other set of machines. I open and close their drawers and check toner settings. I still sense I'm being watched even as I jog up the back stairs.

Each time I glance around me, I don't see anyone who stands out. Every desk is occupied with a frazzled student with their nose in a book or writing in a notebook. It's a common scene two to three times a semester.

I rise after squatting to check the lowest drawer on the machine, and there's someone behind me. I jump with a squeak, and my back hits the machine. My heart races, and my hands curl into fists, ready to strike.

"Shit, Izzy." Mario's eyes widen as he takes me in. "I'm sorry, I didn't mean to scare you."

"Fuck. Shit. Damn it!" I curse one after another as my hand flies to comfort the new ache in my back. "I know, but you did a great job. I'm surprised I didn't piss myself."

Mario raises a brow. "Everything okay?"

"Why on earth would you walk up that close to someone?" I suck in air via my nose, hoping to calm myself. I'm embarrassed and annoyed at this point, but my fear left the moment I recognized Mario.

"Are you hurt?" he asks me, and his hand—his warm and *large* hand—presses against my back. My lady bits stand to attention at his nearness, and hot damn does he smell good. He moves his head back, and we are inches apart.

My heart races for an entirely different reason. "Yeah." I don't even recognize my own voice. It's needy, and my eyes are glued to his mouth. His hand moves to my waist, and I swear the heat is searing through my clothes straight to my skin. I try to step back, but his hold tightens.

"Izzy?"

"Yeah?" I say, leaning into him. My mind is chanting *girlfriend* over and over again, but my body leans toward him with a big "F-you." What the hell is wrong with me?

"I—"

Bang.

We jump apart at the loud noise. My elbow bangs into the metal front that houses the electronics for paying for copies. "Ouch!" I yelp as I look down the aisle and see a student who's dropped a few books.

Mario gently grabs my arm and raises my sleeve to look at my elbow. "You're not having any luck right now, are you?"

"No. And whoever said it's funny when you hit your funny bone needs to be smacked."

He rubs the red spot on my elbow. "This bone up here," he says as his fingers trail along the back of my upper arm, leaving goose bumps along the way. The touch isn't meant to be sexual, but it goes to all the good places. "It's called the humerus. Calling it the funny bone is a pun on the humerus. It's a homophone."

"Oh…" I mutter. "Well, it's not funny at all." I need to get my head on straight because his nearness and touch is scrambling my brain. Except he's not stepping back, and his hand is still on my arm. My eyes roam his face and land on his full lips. No amount of injuries is stopping me from my blatant stare. My morals are slipping from my grasp at an alarming speed.

"Izzy?"

"Mhmm?" I need to stop staring at those kissable lips. They aren't mine to enjoy!

"I was wondering if—"

My phone rings, and it's the tone I've set for the circulation desk. "Sorry, it's Circ, so I need to get this."

"Izzy?"

"Yeah?" I ask, half-listening as Mario steps from me, taking his heat with him.

"No one's in the office, and the schedule says you and Jerry are here. We have a student on the fourth floor who needs some help."

I nod as Mario retreats another step from me. "I'm on my way." My thumb ends the call, and I slip the phone back into my pocket. "Sorry, I need to go help someone."

"That's fine. It can wait." He takes one more step back but stops himself. Before I even realize he's leaned forward, he kisses my cheek and whispers, "I'm sorry I scared you."

I'm stunned silent as Mario walks away. He looks over his shoulder at me one last time and disappears down an aisle. My hand cups my cheek, and I turn toward the set of stairs nearest me. I'm confused over the entire interaction, and he's left me sexually frustrated unlike any other guy. Hell, we haven't even kissed.

Girlfriend! my mind yells.

And yet the butterflies are twisting me into tight knots. Upstairs, I find the group standing around the machine with matching puzzled expressions, and I gather my wits in time to help them. After I've determined they are suffering from an awful case of user error, I check the other machines on the floor.

I catch movement and notice the man from downstairs peeking at me over a book. It's a library, and it could be entirely coincidental, but my internal alarms are blaring at me. I offer a polite smile and decide the elevator is a safer option than the stairs.

With a careful glance over my shoulder, I see the man is following me at a safe distance. "Nope," I mutter to myself and turn into the woman's bathroom. The stalls are empty, and I lock the door. After unlocking my phone, I dial Jerry immediately.

"Hey, what's up?" he asks.

"I'm on the fourth floor in the ladies' restroom next

to the elevators. Can you come up and escort me back down?"

"On my way."

One thing I love about my boss is he's all about safety. After some weird things happened in the library a few years ago, he sat us all down—male and female workers alike. If at any point we were uncomfortable, we were to call him or the front desk. No questions asked. This is the first time I found myself needing to call him. I am probably being dramatic, but my internal alarm is ringing loud and clear. It's better that I feel stupid later than to be explaining to someone what happened to me.

Taking advantage of where I was, I quickly use the restroom and wash my hands. A minute later, I heard a knock on the door.

"Izzy?" Jerry called.

After I unlock the door and step out, I look both ways. I don't see the strange man from earlier. We take the elevator down, and I tell Jerry about the man and the incident. His jaw clenches as he nods. Once we reach the office, he unlocks the door and props it open with the door stop.

"I'm going to take a look around," he tells me before heading back out. We both know I'm safe on the first floor since our office sits within shouting distance of the circulation desk. The chances of Jerry seeing the guy and recognizing him based on my description was a toss-up. There's no point stopping him though.

I've known Jerry since I was in middle school. My sister used to work in this same office when he became her boss. He then eagerly waited for me to graduate high school so he could hire me on. I know he won't do anything reckless or stupid. If he does manage to find the guy, he would send me a picture to confirm it before calling the cops.

It will be hard to prove the man was following me, but oddballs are as common as students in the library.

"Izzy?" a voice snaps, and I can tell it isn't the first time the person has said my name.

My thoughts clear, allowing my eyes and brain to focus once more. "Sorry?"

"Are you okay?" Mario asks.

What's Mario doing in here? He never comes in here.

"I'm fine," I say automatically and push to my feet. "Does someone need help?" I try to ignore the way my face has warmed to Mario's appearance.

"No one needs help, at least not that I know of. Are you sure you're okay? It took me quite a bit to get your attention, and it doesn't seem like you."

I cock my head to the side. "Not like me?" I sound like an idiot. I'm unable to form a sentence now that he's around again. His brows are furrowed together with worry, and his eyes are intensely focused. I watch as they travel down my body. It's not in a sexual or creepy way either. Concern is evident in his features; his gaze is an exploration of me for injuries.

"Okay…" His eyes move to the clock and back to mine. "I was wondering when you got off."

"I—uh—" I say, startled by his question. Sure, he kissed my cheek not even an hour ago, but I'm still processing Mario talking to me for more than a brief interaction in the break room.

Jerry strolls in. "I didn't see him, Izzy—Oh, hey, Mario! How are you doing? How do you like it at Reference?"

I look between both men. Jerry talks to everyone he sees and meets, so I'm not entirely surprised by his easy chatter.

Mario nods. "Hi, Jerry! I'm doing well, and I really

like it over there. I submitted for an internship. Who didn't you see?"

"This creep who was following Izzy. From how she described him, I know I've seen him here before." Jerry scratches the back of his head, and his eyes gloss over as he thinks hard on the matter.

Mario straightens as his body stiffens with the information. "Someone was following you?"

I shrug. "Probably a coincidence—"

"Izzy, you've never called me like that. You're level-headed, and if you thought he was following you, I would bet my retirement on the fact that he was indeed following you," Jerry says in his fatherly, don't-argue-with-me voice.

My shoulders slump. I rub my face. The adrenaline from earlier is waning, and I don't have the energy to put up a fight. Jerry isn't wrong, and I really don't think it's in my head. It's just weird having another person—Mario specifically—hear that Jerry needed to rescue me from the bathroom.

"Why don't you go get some fresh air? I can hold down the fort." Jerry motions to Mario, causing me to look up.

"Let's go get some coffee," Mario tells me, and I pull out my wallet from inside my backpack. "Leave it. It's my treat."

Jerry gives a satisfied nod and sits in his chair. My feet move automatically, and as I reach the door, he calls out, "Take your time!"

CHAPTER 13

Mario's warm hand presses against my lower back, and I look up into his chocolate-brown eyes. They're molten, and I'm pretty sure I could get lost in them. "This way. Let's get out of the building."

A light breeze blows, and I breathe him in. He smells so good, and I'm tempted to press my face against him for another whiff. We walk in silence as we pass other students on the path. I don't know what to say to him. I'm crazy attracted to him and have been for a while, but he has a girlfriend. Although, it leaves me wondering why his hand is still touching my back. Why did he come in the office, and why did he kiss my cheek? So many whys, and I'm exhausted and flustered.

"How's your girlfriend?" I blurt, and my face warms. It's easily the fastest I've gone red in a very long time. "I'm sorry. I didn't mean—"

Mario chuckles, and the sound warms me for an entirely different reason. "Don't have one," he says, his eyes staring at my mouth before he looks up to see where we are going.

"You don't?"

"Nope. Do you—um—have a boyfriend?" he asks, his confidence wavering for a second.

"No."

Mario nods but remains quiet for another minute. The silence between us isn't awkward. If anything, it allows me to think and accept the attraction between us. I am more excited than I should be by the news that he doesn't have a girlfriend.

"What would you like to drink?" he asks, and I notice we're inside the coffee shop. Only two sets of students are in front of us, by some miracle. I look at the board and bite my lip as I narrow it down to two options. A small groan sounds from my side, and I find Mario's intently staring at my mouth.

"What?" I ask, my voice breathless. I bite down on the corner of my mouth.

His thumb reaches between us and releases my lip. "Nothing."

"How can I help you?" the man behind the counter asks, breaking our staring contest.

My nipples are pressing against my bra, and I squeeze my thighs together. I tell the clerk my order, and we stand to the side after Mario pays.

"Thanks again," I say and nod toward the drinks.

He shrugs, and I notice he's caught a case of the nerves. "My pleasure."

With our drinks in hand, we look around for a place to sit. Students are sprawled across every surface. Some quite literally, while they take a nap on the table with their things everywhere. I notice a girl as she leaves a love seat, and I glance at Mario. He nods, and we head over. I can't help but note how much of the last fifteen minutes has been spent using nonverbal cues—not in an uncomfortable way but rather the way you see your parents when they just *get* each other.

Mario puts his arm out, ushering me to sit first. This works out for me because I watch his jeans curl around his ass when he bends down. I need to check that ass out more often.

The left side of his body presses against my right, and my heart races at the contact. I blow on my drink and sip, hoping it will calm my crazy nerves. I don't think I was this nervous around any of my dates.

"Did you know the guy who was following you?" he asks, breaking the silence.

I shake my head and take another sip. "No. I don't know him, but I've seen him around." Something in my mind clicks. "He came in the other day to staple some papers. He handed me a card for a talent scout."

Mario's brow raises. "Talent scout?"

"Yeah, he thinks I should be in the *biz*."

He turns a little and studies me from top to bottom. "Izzy, it's no secret you're gorgeous. I don't know I would trust him on the talent scout part. Did he have a card? Did you get his name? Did he offer any reputable sources he's worked with? I don't know, I just—why are you smiling at me like that?"

"Thank you, and I'm going to try to not be offended since we don't really know each other…"

"But?" he asks.

"But you don't know me. I don't exactly trust people blindly. Sure, it was nice to hear him say he thought I was pretty enough to go for it, but I'm not dumb. I took the card he gave me of the talent scout, and I did my research. Then, do you want to know what I did?" I whisper the last part.

Mario narrows his eyes, but the way his lips twitch tells me he sees right through me. "What?"

"I ripped it up and threw it away," I shrug and take another sip as he chuckles. What a sweet sound it is. This man, who I know as well as the last few men I've dated, affects me in a new and interesting way. Well, then again, I did get to know Zeke better than the others. Too bad I didn't know about his twitch or how fond he was of his dick until it was too late.

"You got me. I'm sorry. I shouldn't have assumed."

"No, you shouldn't have, but unfortunately, we both know that gimmick will work on many girls. I just hope he's harmless enough. Although it creeped the hell out of me when I found him watching and trailing me."

"I bet it did. So, um, you said you didn't have a boyfriend. What happened with the guy a few weeks back?"

"Who, Zeke?"

Mario shrugs. "Maybe? You were heading out with him."

I nod. "Probably Zeke. Well, we'd been seeing each other, but I ended it over a month ago."

"You ended it? What happened?"

I stare at Mario. I haven't talked this much with him before, and now suddenly I'm in a coffee shop discussing my sucky dating life with him. Looking at my cup, I think of where to start.

Mario's hand cups my knee. "I'm sorry. You don't have to tell me anything."

His hand is heavy and warm. What would it be like if he ran it up my thigh? Massaging the muscles until he cupped my center? The thoughts pass through my mind quickly. My breath is lodged in my throat, and I know if I touch myself right now, I'd be wet. My core tightens as my imagination changes my hand to his. I haven't ever been this wound up. An orgasm is waiting around the corner all because his hand heated my skin, and my dirty imagination ran with it.

Mario squeezes my thigh where it meets my knee.

"Izzy? Are you okay?"

Parting my lips, I gulp in a breath to alleviate the burn from depriving my lungs of oxygen. "Yeah." I meet his eyes and watch them dilate in reaction to my own.

His thumb rubs back and forth, an innocent and comforting touch, but this time I can see he's testing us both. "I didn't mean to upset you."

I take another deep breath and smile. "I'm not upset. We haven't spoken many words to each other outside the break room, and now suddenly..." The warm coffee calms me when I take another sip.

"You're right. I was just... curious I guess," he says and removes his hand.

I frown at the loss of his touch. I liked his hand there. It belonged and was exciting. "Things just didn't work out with Zeke. It seems I suck at picking guys."

Mario smiles, and I see he's biting back a chuckle. "Dating sucks in general. I doubt it's you picking awful guys."

I laugh full belly laughs at his comment. "Challenge accepted!"

He chuckles. "Oh, yeah?" His eyes sparkle with amusement, and I can't believe it makes him look more handsome than usual. "Shoot! I can't wait to hear these."

Pressing the power button to my cell phone, I wait for the screen to illuminate to check the time. "I need to get back soon, so here's a short, short version." I turn to my side and face him. My right knee presses against his hip, and my shin lies flat against the side of his leg. Mario turns and mimics my positions, so our legs mirror each other. "Okay, I'll work backward and mention the most memorable ones," I say and wink.

"This sounds like it's going to be good." He chuckles and waves his hand for me to start.

"Zeke was nice enough. So nice, I decided to sleep

with him."

Mario's eyes darken, and his jaw clamps shut at my words, but he remains silent.

"The man wouldn't shut up about his dick. Talked it up the whole time even though I was a done deal." I'm sorely tempted to mention the man's tic but decide to keep it to myself.

"He talked it up?"

"Yeah! Not a normal 'hey look at how big I am.' Almost like he wanted me to know how lucky I was that I'd be having sex with him. It was so weird."

"You're exaggerating!"

"I wish I was. Then there was Robert. He liked to send me pictures of himself nude in the shower."

"Oh, I remember seeing Robert," Mario says, and I recall the way he ran out of the breakroom after the text popped up.

"That's right! Well, he's divorced with two kids. At least, that's what he told me." I raise an eyebrow and offer Mario an I-don't-believe-his-shit kind of look.

"What a dick!"

"Yup! Saw him while I was out with Zeke one night. Then there was Brad. He snuck out before the bill arrived, effectively sticking me with a four-hundred-dollar check after ordering expensive Italian food and wine. Tristan wanted to screw me in the public bathroom after a couple hours of chatting and then there was Johnny." I sigh. "Johnny was a sweetheart, very good looking, funny—"

"What went wrong with him?" Mario asks, fully engaged in my disastrous dating life.

"He couldn't kiss for shit."

Mario chuckles. "You dumped a guy because he wasn't great at kissing?"

My brows snap together at his judgment. Determined

and without thinking, my hand curls around Mario's neck and pulls him to me. I run my lips along his, testing, teasing until his part. Our tongues caress, and we explore each other's mouths. The kiss is... divine. Nearly losing my train of thought, I focus on the point I want to make. Changing directions, I stab my tongue toward his throat and do everything I can to recreate Johnny's kiss. Mario pulls back, his eyes wide in horror as he wipes his mouth.

His mouth opens to speak, but he shuts it before a word escapes. I stare at his lips and know I can't end things at that. I've already crossed a line but hell if I'll let him go on thinking it's how *I* kiss. Leaning forward, I watch him, and I brush my lips over his tentatively. My tongue lightly strokes his full lips before I nibble on the flesh. His eyes flutter closed, and his hand cups my head. I deepen the kiss and melt into his touch.

Mario's kisses are better than anything I've ever experienced. Before I can forget where we are, I end it with another chaste kiss. We stare at each other for a minute. I memorize the feel of his soft, full lips on mine. His thumb rubs against the apple of my cheek, and it takes everything in me not to press my face against his palm.

I clear my throat. "That last kiss was—"

"Amazing..."

I nod. "Yeah, now imagine if the first kiss happened every... single... time?"

His eyes widen. "I—I don't know what the hell that was, but I thought you were trying to—"

"Drown you? Suffocate you?"

He chuckles. "Yes! Once I got past the shock that you were kissing me, I was enjoying it and then... then *that!*"

"Yup, and *that* is how you dump someone for being a bad kisser. No matter how great they are, you can't risk your life."

Mario chuckles. "No, you really shouldn't." His eyes drop to my lips, and he captures them in a sweet kiss. A slow burn lights in my stomach and spreads through my body. I sigh, lost in his touch. He peppers me with a short burst of kisses before he speaks. "Have dinner with me, Izzy."

I gaze into his eyes. My mind short-circuits under his attention, the reminder that I wouldn't go on another date not far behind. Then again, when I told myself I was done dating, I was specifically thinking about that awful site. Sure, I know it's brought some couples together like my cousin and her husband, but for me, Izabella Rae Daniels, it has brought me nothing but grief.

Mario rubs my lower lip with his thumb and waits. He doesn't seem upset at the amount of time it is taking me to answer him. His handsome face is so close to mine, and the heat of his body warms me at all the points we touch.

I nod, a short one as a tremble runs down my body. I'm taking this chance, and I hope it won't go up in flames. Not only have I admired this man from afar, we work in the same building. This could spell trouble in quite a few ways for me.

"I need to hear the words, princess."

My head cocks to the side at the endearment. "Princess?"

He blushes as he looks past me. "If you say yes, I promise to explain?"

I smile as I nod. "Okay, deal. Mario?"

"Yeah?"

"I'd love to hear why you just called me princess during dinner." I watch his eyes crinkle in pleasure. The joy that fills me at his expression is different. I enjoy making others happy, but there's something about the way I puff up with pride at his pleased response.

"Great! How about I walk you back to the office, and we can decide where you'd like to eat. I hear Italian places are out of the equation?"

I slap his arm playfully with indignation. "Really?"

"Too soon?" he jokes as we walk side by side out of the coffee shop.

"Yes, too soon!" I laugh. "Don't take joy out of my miserable dates!"

He grabs a strand of my hair and playfully tugs it. "I'm sorry they were so awful, but I'm not sorry you're single."

His words hit me in the gut where I've been all jittery since the moment I saw him this morning. I decide to not address his words and instead start the get-to-know-you stage while we walk our way back.

CHAPTER 14

"What do you mean you have a date tonight?" Val asks as she puts on a pair of dangly earrings. "I thought you deleted the app? Please tell me you didn't download it again."

I sit on the edge of her bed and lean back on my elbows. "I didn't. Where are you going?"

"Not talking about me, Izabella!" she scolds.

"Well damn, why am I getting the full name? I take it you're meeting up with Mason?" I ask, saying his name in a singsong voice.

She glares, but I see she's freaking out. Her head bows down as she looks around the dresser, and I push off the bed. I wrap my arms around her waist in a hug. Val's body trembles. "I'm scared," she whispers.

"I know, honey. You really like him, don't you?" I whisper back. Her eyes meet mine in the mirror, and I see the tiniest of nods. "Look." I turn her around. I grab her hands in mine and squeeze them. "If he breaks your heart, I'll break his legs."

She laughs, and a single tear rolls down her cheek. "I love you, Izzy."

"I love you too! Now go out, have fun, and don't punish him for something he never did," I say and kiss her cheek.

Val takes a deep, shuddering breath, and I know I did my job as her best friend when she smiles. "Okay. Are you going to tell me this guy's name at least?"

I grin. "Mario."

"That name sounds familiar," she says, her eyes squinting in thought.

"Go, before you're late. If there is anything to tell after tonight, we'll get some ice cream and dish."

"Deal, but if you need me, just call. It doesn't matter if I'm out or not." She hugs me tightly.

"Ditto."

When we hear a knock at the door, her face lights up. She hurries past me, and with a little wave, she leaves for her date. I enter my room and head straight for the closet. Mario let me choose where we would eat, and I picked a local Tex-Mex joint near campus. I knew it would be busy, but I also loved their chimichangas.

I pick a spaghetti-strap shirt and flowy black skirt to go with a cute pair of wedge sandals. I've gone on so many dates this year, and I'm tired of trying to impress. I brush my hair out before weaving it into a loose over-the-shoulder braid. I aim for casual and comfortable, and I must admit I look beautiful in my simple ensemble.

I'm not big into makeup. It's not that I don't have it, I just don't want to go through all the trouble. Something about Mario makes me want to go natural. I swipe the mascara wand over my lashes and a pretty pink gloss on my lips and call it good. Earrings matching the ones Valerie wore for her date hang from my ears, and some silver bangles slide up and down my wrist.

Seeing the time, I grab my clutch and keys and leave the apartment. I probably took twenty minutes to get ready, including the shower I took before I chatted with Val. Even though Mario insisted on picking me up, I stuck to my guns and declined. First dates were always the hardest, and I was more comfortable having an exit strategy.

The parking lot in the front is full when I arrive. I find a spot around the side, not too far back, and park. I'm jittery with nerves as I work my way to the door. There are so many ways this could end badly. I hate the fact I've even thought of a few of them.

Can I really stay on this crappy dating streak? Oh wait, did I just jinx myself? Maybe I should turn and leave now before this date tops the others.

Mario steps outside, and in his hand is one large red hibiscus flower. His smile is bright when he spots me, and his eyes skim down my body. He takes his time as I walk up, and when I'm a few feet away, he meets my eyes. "You look beautiful."

He's wearing a dark pair of jeans and an untucked long-sleeve dress shirt. The look is semi-casual and perfect for our first date. I take in the way he fills in the shirt throughout the chest. "You look handsome yourself."

"Here, this is for you." Mario offers the flower, and our fingers brush as I grab it. Butterflies take flight in my stomach at the innocent touch.

"Thank you." I tuck it behind my ear. "How do I look?" I ask playfully.

"Perfect," he mutters and takes another second to admire me. "Ready to eat?"

"Yes! I'm starving."

Mario's the perfect gentleman. He opens the door for me, allows me to order first, insists on paying, lets me pick the seat, doesn't sit until I do... I'm rather floored. None of his behavior seems forced or for show. If it is, he's a damn good actor.

We sit with our drinks and make small talk. Mario listens to what I have to say, and his focus is directed solely on me—not the way some people hear you but don't truly listen. When he laughs, a warmth spreads along my body, and I can't wait to hear the sound again.

"So, um…" I say, nervous to ask, but my curiosity is killing me.

Mario leans forward. "Spit it out."

I laugh. "Sorry, I want to know something, but I don't want to ruin the mood or upset you."

He grabs my hand resting on the table. It's a simple act meant to soothe my nerves, but it makes my heart race. "Izzy, if you have something on your mind, I want to know about it."

"Okay. I was wondering about your girlfriend. What happened?"

"Ah." He grins. "I see why you're nervous. Her name is Missy, and I ended it a few weeks ago."

"Can I ask why?"

Mario looks away and rubs the back of his neck with his free hand. He's visibly uncomfortable, and I don't like what I've done.

"Never mind, you don't need to answer."

He shook his head. "No, it's okay. We'd been together for a couple years. Things… changed. I didn't feel the same way about her as she did about me. For the last six months of our relationship, I was going through the motions, and it wasn't fair to her or me."

I squeeze his hands, and he meets my eyes. "I'm sorry. It must have been hard."

He nods. "Thanks. People change, and we realize we want different things in life. To be honest, it was me more than her. I couldn't be the guy she wanted, and I was tired of trying."

The sadness in his voice clogs my throat. When I asked the question, I didn't know what he would say, but I didn't expect to be affected by his words. We are still rather young as we are entering our mid-twenties. Life hasn't had the opportunity to deal us many shitty cards. I've met a few people who lived through things you only hear of on TV, but they are the minority.

"I can see you still love her from your words, but you can only be you."

He studies my face and smiles. "I haven't been in love with Missy for a long time."

We eat in comfortable silence, only mentioning the food or noting how busy the place has become. After the heavy turn in our conversation, I take the time to reflect on his words. All things considered, this date is topping off the others.

"Why are you smiling?" Mario asks as he pushes his empty plate to the side.

My cheeks warm. He's been rather open with me, and there isn't any reason to not admit the truth. "I'm realizing how much I'm enjoying my time with you. This is easily the best date I've gone on in a long time."

He chuckles. "If that's the case, then you're very easy to please. It doesn't sound like those others were worth their salt if a simple meal and conversations about my ex is better."

I shrug. "Maybe it's just my company?"

His smile is warm, and my heart races at the way he looks at me. "Are you done?" he asks with a nod to my empty plate.

"Yup." We stare at each other a few moments. I met him here, so if we decide to prolong this date, I'll either have to meet him at the next place or take a chance.

"How would you like to go people-watching?"

My head cocks to the side. Of all the things he could

suggest, people-watching wasn't even close to what I considered. Go to the movies, a casino, or even his place—but not that. "I love people-watching. It's right after my love of reading."

"Great." He stands and offers me his hand. It's warm and larger than my own. "I know you wanted to drive here separately, and I don't blame you." Here it comes... "Do you mind driving? That way if you become uncomfortable, you can leave, and I'll just take an Uber back here."

I make a conscious effort to not let my surprise show but fail. From the expression on his face, he realizes it too. We work our way to the door. His hand is on the small of my back, and he's a step behind as we maneuver around the people waiting to eat. "Yeah, that works for me. You sure you're okay with a woman driving?" I ask over my shoulder.

He chuckles. "I don't mind a woman in control," he whispers against my ear, startling me. Mario leans past me and pushes the door open. When I look back at him, he winks. I have no clever reply, as the double meaning of his words wreak havoc with my libido.

First date, Izabella! It doesn't matter if he's sweet, funny, or sex on a stick. Stick to the plan!

CHaPTer 15

The temperature has dropped a little since we arrived, but it's great on my warm skin. I blush enough as it is, and with Mario's words, I relish the cool air. I guide us to my car, and he opens my door before going around to the passenger side.

I giggle, and he stares after shutting his door. "What?"

"No one's opened the door for me when I'm the one driving."

He buckles himself. "It gave me an excuse to stay close to you."

I freeze a second after putting the car in reverse. He's free with his words, and I honestly can't figure out if it's a charming ploy or him being frank. "Where to?" I ask, unable to address his words—if there is even anything to say.

Mario suggests we go downtown, and our conversation switches to our families and how we ended up in Las Vegas. "Dad was stationed here while I was in high school. I was given the opportunity to graduate here instead of leaving during my senior year, so I did."

I nod, enjoying the pieces of himself he shares with me. "When my parents divorced, Mom moved us here— close enough we could still see Dad but she could also afford being a single parent here. It blows my mind how people can even try to live in California."

Mario shares as much as I do, and I find it refreshing. So many guys shut off and only participate in the conversation when they are required. He doesn't complain about my music being on pop; he listens and tells jokes. He's an easy-going person who puts me at ease. Sure, my eyes keep landing on his mouth when I catch glimpses of him. I'm quite aware of the sexual chemistry filling the car, but I'm relaxed as well as anyone can be with someone they are attracted to.

Let me tell you, I'm ridiculously attracted to him. I have seen him on and off around the library for months. There wasn't any way I couldn't notice him. He's tall, dark, and handsome to a T. I never thought he would be interested in me. He did have a girlfriend as well, but now he's single, and I'm single. Will he live up to the version of him I've created in my mind?

I cut the engine after parking in a garage, and the music plays quietly as it waits for me to open the door. I don't hear it. My heart thunders in my ears as the oxygen in the car seems to disappear. I'm surrounded by Mario. His presence fills the space. Gone is my relaxed state, and in its place? Tension. Hot, pure, pulsing sexual tension.

I glance at him and notice his eyes are darker, almost black in contrast to his normally chocolate-colored eyes. A shiver runs through me at the way he watches me. I told myself I wouldn't have sex tonight, but if he asks me now, I'll throw all caution to the wind.

My legs straddling his hips as I kiss the hell out of him… His hands cupping my ass before pulling my shirt and bra down, so my breasts spill over into his hands…

His hard dick straining through his jeans for my center...

"Princess, if you keep looking at me like that, I'm going to lose all control," he warns, his voice gravelly with desire.

I bite my lip and blush. Swallowing past the lump in my throat, my eyes flick to his mouth—a pretty mouth with full lips that I haven't kissed since the coffee shop.

His hands frame my face. "One taste," he whispers and then his mouth is on mine.

He devours me. His tongue strokes and tastes mine. There is no slow tease of lips brushing each other. The kiss is deep and hot. I whimper in pleasure and note my lungs burn with their need for oxygen. Holy shit! Never has a man kissed me so thoroughly—raw unrestrained passion in one kiss.

Sucking in his lower lip, I relish the taste of its plump flesh when Mario groans. He ends the kiss and presses his forehead against mine. Our labored breaths are harsh and loud in the now-silent car.

One hand moves to the side of my neck, and his thumb presses on my jaw, forcing me to meet his eyes. They are as shocked and confused as I'm sure mine are. One thing is for sure; we have explosive chemistry between us. The man knows how to use his mouth. I'm putty in his hands and can only imagine how much better it can be between us.

He kisses me again, this one a soft brush of his lips along mine. "We better go before I forget my manners," he whispers.

Moving back to his seat, the delicious scent of his cologne wafts away from me, and I long for him to be close. Mario steps out, his sexy ass pointed toward me. I watch his arm move in front of him and hear the barest of groans as he adjusts himself. The door closes, and I can't move. I try my damnedest to calm down, pressing my thighs together, which not only doesn't help but makes it worse.

One kiss and I ache like never before.

Mario opens my door, and I accept his offered hand. He kisses my cheek, and his fingers link with mine. It's comfortable and natural, faster than I'm used to, but with Mario it just *works*.

"Where to, princess?" His words are gentle, and I think it rattles me more.

"You never did explain 'princess.'"

He chuckles and squeezes my hand in his. "You lead, I talk?"

"Deal," I agree and guide us toward the elevators.

He sighs. "Please don't think I'm a jerk, okay?"

My brows crease. "Okay?"

"I've noticed you for a long time now. In the last six months, every time we've run into each other in the breakroom?" He pauses, and I nod, encouraging him to continue. "I kind of did it on purpose."

I think on his admission, still unsure how this relates to him calling me princess. "You were following me? Weren't you with Missy during that time?" I'm not sure if I should be creeped out or flattered or what.

He presses the down button on the elevator and stands in front of me. "I wasn't following you around like some weird stalker, so please don't think that. I was attracted to you, and yes, I shouldn't have been because I was with Missy. The first time I bumped into you in the break room was on accident. I spent all day thinking about you and that was only after a couple minutes around you."

The elevator dings, and we step on. We remain silent as we stand side by side next to a couple. Mario has been attracted to me for months? I need a drink to process this information, so as soon as the elevator doors open, I pull us toward a bar I like.

Mario opens his mouth, and I place a finger to his lips. "Nope. Drinks first."

"Okay." He guides me to two free stools facing the walkway where we can watch the tired tourists stroll by.

The waitress flits over and takes our orders before checking a few guests on her way to the bar. I redirect my attention to the crowd and laugh when a man dressed as cupid pretends to shoot an arrow at us.

Mario laughs. "I swear he's always here."

I nod. "I've seen him a few times."

We point different people out as we talk and laugh before the beer appears. Mario pays for the round, and the waitress ambles off as I swallow a mouthful. He's ready to burst with more information, and I know it's coming. I bite my tongue, forcing myself to give him the time he needs.

He lifts his glass. "This is a good one."

"Yeah, it's one of my favorites."

We become silent as Mario stares into the amber liquid. When his eyes meet mine, they are open windows. "I couldn't stop thinking about you, Izzy. I hated myself for it because I was with Missy. There you were, this beautiful woman I was crazy attracted to, but I had no right to be when I was with someone else. You were this princess I could only watch from afar and talk to during our short coffee chats. I never got the impression you were being anything more than nice with me, so I was stuck."

I nod, unable to say anything as I let him unload. This conversation would have been better in a private setting, but as he confesses these things, everyone around us falls away. I'm surprised and flattered by his admission. I'd noticed him for a while now, but I too didn't think it was mutual attraction since he was with

Missy.

"At first, I chalked it up to the fact you're gorgeous, and I was simply attracted to you," he says. "Over time, the little bit we chatted left me wanting more. When I saw you were in fact dating someone, I wanted to be the man taking you out. At that point, I realized how unfair I was being to Missy and myself. Regardless of whether I got a chance to date you, I needed to let her go. She deserves to have a chance at happiness even if I was stuck as a commoner watching the princess from a far."

"So not because you think I'm some spoiled girl, but—"

"Because you're like a princess I couldn't fathom I'd get a chance with," he whispers before drinking deeply from his beer.

His words are sweet. No man has looked at me like he does. It's exhilarating and makes me think of the romance novels I read. Only they're fiction, completely concocted from the author's mind. No way would I experience some of those things.

Pushing aside those thoughts, I relax as the beer takes effect, and our conversation moves to safer topics. We make up stories about some of the characters we see and order another round that Mario insists on buying. I don't mind paying, but I'm also not going to raise a stink over his insistence.

We talk about everything and more. Mario is obsessed with some of the classics I won't touch after being forced to read in high school. He's in the process of completing the last leg of his library sciences degree, and as he'd told Jerry, he's trying to get an internship in the Reference Department.

Before I know it, I'm yawning behind my hand. "I'm so sorry."

Mario looks at his watch. "It's late. Let's get going.

If you'd like, I can walk you to your car and then I'll just call a car. That way, you can get straight to bed?"

I narrow my eyes. "Umm… no. I can drive you back. I'm not very tired, and I've been drinking water for the last hour and half, so I'm good. It's been a long day, so I apologize."

His fingers link with mine, and he looks at me. "Okay."

When we make it to my car, Mario walks me to my door and pins me to it. Thigh to thigh, his arms cage me in, and he thickens against my belly. The glass is cold on my back, opposite of his warmth pressing on my front. He stares at my mouth, and I run my tongue along my dry lips.

Mario's groan vibrates through me before he cups my face and kisses me. His lips are soft and firm against mine. They rub mine with ease, and his tongue slides smoothly across. I sigh, and he deepens our kiss.

My arms slide up his chest, enjoying the journey across his firm muscles before locking behind his neck. I pull him to me, and my breasts flatten against him. Our tongues caress in a slow rhythmic dance that sends heat flooding between my thighs.

I'm moaning into his mouth, considering if I should wrap my legs around his waist. If I lose my mind so easily with him in a darkened parking garage, I'll be in trouble later if this turns into more.

He breaks our kiss, and his lips leave a trail along my cheek and down my exposed neck. His leg presses between mine, and my hips buck, looking for friction to ease the ache building in my sex. All logical thought has left my mind as our kiss becomes too sexy for public eyes.

Mario grabs my hips and holds them still. His breath blows down my chest when he presses his forehead to my shoulder and pants. "I lose control with you."

I cup the back of his neck, willing my heart to slow. My body is flushed with desire, and I'm sure I match the color of my shirt. Mario pulls from me and opens my door. Without a word, I get in and he shuts it. Taking a deep breath, I rub my arms. They're cold now that he's not warming my front. His door opens, and he slides in. We sit for a moment, neither speaking as we try to catch our breath.

Once my brain can function, I drive us to Mario's car. Somewhere along the drive, he's grabbed my hand. His thumb runs along my knuckles, and I smile over at him. Of all the dates I've experienced in the last year, I have to say, tonight was the best.

CHAPTER 16

"Who are you texting?" Val asks.

She's next to me on the couch, and we have our drinks and snacks ready for a movie night. To be honest, I don't even know what we're about to watch. I told her to pick since I've been distracted chatting with Mario. From the dirty look directed at me, I need to set my phone aside.

"Mario. What did you pick?" I ask and point at the TV.

"How the hell do you two have anything left to say?" she asks as the previews start.

I grab some peanuts. "Why do they even leave this shit in the DVD versions?"

"They do it so I can ask you again how you have anything left to say and not worry I'm missing the beginning of the movie."

I laugh. "Geez, woman, touchy." I unlock my phone and look at the texts. "Um, right now he's telling me about a guy they found watching porn on one of the back computers of the main floor." I lock the phone and set it aside again.

"Hey, Mario is the one with the cryptic message about his coffee, right?" she asks with a raised brow.

I had completely forgotten about that incident and nod. "Yeah, something about the color suiting me? That's a weird thing to remember."

"And his skin tone matches the color of your coffee, no?" Val asks, ignoring the latter.

I rub my forehead, allowing the memory to come forward. "Yeah?"

"It was a complicated way to tell you he wanted to be with you!" she says, excited she had been right with her initial assessment.

At that time, I still believed he was taken. "While it may have been clever, it went right over my head. Left me pretty damn confused too. Men!" We chuckle and nod in agreement. "How's Mason?"

"He's good." Her eyes slide to mine. "I hope you don't mind, but he's staying the night after he gets off work."

I shake my head. "You mean he's going to be getting off work and getting off with you?"

"Shut up and watch the movie," she says and bursts into a fit of giggles.

I wake up to a knock at our door and realize we both fell asleep on the couch. Looking through the hole, I recognize Mason and let him in. "She's on the couch snoring."

He chuckles. "Sorry it's so late. I texted her to see if she wanted me to go home, but now I know why she never replied to my message."

Val turns on the couch and rubs the sleep from her eyes as I grab my things. "Good night, you two," I tell them and head for my room.

Thanks to the mini nap during the movie, I'm wide awake. I grab my tablet, get comfy under the covers, and return to my book. I'm not sure how long I've been reading when I hear Val and Mason in the next room. Their deep moans pierce the wall, and my mind goes to Mario. It's been a week since our first date, and we've seen each other nearly every day at work.

A few times, we snuck in kisses in the breakroom. Other times, we texted each other to meet in the staircase at the back of the library. Every time our mouths meet, I swear my body lights on fire. His kisses are addictive, and the thought alone causes my body to react.

The erotic sounds mix with the memories of all the heavy petting between Mario and me. I set my tablet aside, and my fingers slip under my panties. I'm slick with excitement and imagine it's Mario's hand. His fingers dip inside me, and his thumb finds my clit. Running his fingers around my sensitive bundle of nerves, his mouth latches onto my nipple.

I pluck away, my fantasy guiding me, and within moments my back is arching, and I'm coming. My mouth is dry, and my breaths are ragged. If possible, I'm needier than before I pleasured myself.

I roll off the bed and pad to the bathroom to clean up. Tonight isn't the first night I've heard Val having sex, but it's the first time I've touched myself. I debate for a second whether I should be ashamed before pushing it aside. Getting off to their sounds is comparable to turning on porn. Better even, since I know the woman wasn't faking shit.

Mason and Val are an attractive couple. I'm glad she's allowed herself to get to this next level with him—a reminder I could eventually take things further with Mario even after what happened with Zeke.

On cue, my phone vibrates on the night stand.

Mario: Good night, princess.
Izzy: Good night, handsome.

***

"Where are we going?" I ask, watching the scenery go by.

Mario chuckles and kisses the back of my hand. "I told you it's a surprise, princess."

I never tire hearing him use this new-to-me nickname. I've never been a big fan of pet names, but this one from Mario? I want to swoon. He's so damn sweet, even now when he's driving me crazy by keeping me out of the loop.

"Are we almost there?"

"Yes, now calm down, and tell me about your day."

I laugh and find myself relaxing in my seat as I do just that. Neither of us have much left before graduation, and I'm on the hunt for internships that can put me in a casino. I sit up and turn toward him when I remember something.

He laughs. "Whoa! What's going on?"

"Do you remember when that guy followed me around?"

Mario's face darkens. "Yeah. Don't tell me he's back around."

His eyes move from the road to me a few times, worry etched deeply into his features from his concern. My chest squeezes, and I lean forward and kiss his cheek. "No. Jerry found out a student was using a classroom without permission for 'auditions,'" I told him with air quotes. "Turns out his father used to be an agent, and he's been on campus harassing some of the female students."

"So the guy who approached you is the father of a student?"

"Yeah."

"Wow, that's absurd. Did anyone get hurt?"

I swallow past the lump in my throat. "A couple female students have come forth with rape allegations. The police are expecting more to come out and add to the charges."

"Bastards," Mario growls. He kisses my hand again. "I'm really happy nothing happened to you, Izabella."

I smile and lean my head on his shoulder, sighing when he kisses the top of my head. "I am too. Good thing I listened to my inner voice."

"Good thing," he whispers, his hot breath warming the top of my head.

After a few minutes in silence, I sit up when my neck begins to cramp. "You still aren't going to tell me?"

Mario laughs. "You're such a baby!"

"Don't be mean," I say jokingly as he exits. "Oh! Are we close?"

He squeezes my hand. "Yes!" At the end of the ramp, he sets my hand on his thigh, and I know he hears the little gasp that escapes. We've kept things under control these last few weeks, but I don't know how much more I can take. Mario's kisses and innocent touches arouse me beyond belief. Touching his thigh makes me want to explore, to see if I'm not the only one affected.

He's been a gentleman in terms of sex. We've behaved like horny teenagers, but I'm about to lose my mind. I want more. Need more. What if this is all for naught, and he ends up having some weird thing like Zeke or Johnny? I know I shouldn't compare them. Honestly, the others don't measure up to Mario. I'm only afraid something will happen that will be a deal breaker for me. Before the other two, I didn't realize how quickly it could happen.

"Princess," Mario warns.

Looking down, I see my hand has inched toward the large bulge in his pants. My face inflames, and I retract my hand quickly. "Sorry," I whisper.

He parks and turns toward me. Mario cups my cheek, and his warm palm lightly presses until I meet his eyes. They are dark with desire, nearly black pits. My nipples pucker, and my core tenses at the passion staring back.

"I didn't mean to embarrass you," he whispers. "I can barely keep my hands off you as it is, and I don't want to rush things. I've enjoyed our time together, and I don't want to ruin it by pushing too hard, too fast."

I nod, unable to form words. At least one of us is thinking clearly.

"Ready to have some fun?"

My mind returns to the gutter. Hell yeah I want to have some fun.

Mario groans. "Damn it, princess. I'm not going to be able to walk if you keep looking at me like that."

I force myself to say something. "Sorry."

He chuckles. "No, I don't think you are." He kisses me, and I whimper when he cuts it short. Passion clouds my vision, obscuring all rational thought. I really don't care about his surprise right now. I want him to drive us somewhere private, so we can put ourselves out of our misery.

I startle when my car door opens, and his hand appears. "Come on, let's go inside where it's safe."

"Safe? What, am I going to attack you?" I ask, raising my eyebrow at him.

He chuckles. "Maybe you will. Maybe I'll like it. Maybe, just maybe, it's me you should be worried about."

Shaking my head, I link my fingers with his, and we walk. "You're no fun, just so we're clear about that."

His lips meet my ear. "Princess, I'll show you fun."

I gasp and my muscles clench. "Don't be a tease!"

Mario kisses my cheek and pulls us down the street a

little faster. When I can see past the fog of my sexual frustration, I see a familiar sign ahead. "Really, Dave and Buster's?"

His boyish smile is adorable. The energy around him changes, and I realize I'm becoming addicted to how expressive Mario is.

"Yeah! Have you been here before?"

I shake my head. "Actually, no. I've always wanted to go, but I've never had the chance."

Mario stops in his tracks with an incredulous look on his face. "That's nuts. You've been missing out, and I promise you this is going to be great!"

Inside, we pay, or I should say Mario pays because he refuses to let me. We decide on food first and order at the bar. Flashing lights reflect in the mirror behind the bar and bells and whistles fill the air as a variety of people partake in the games. This almost reminds me of a casino floor, but there's joy in the air rather than the edgy stress that comes with losing your money.

Mario tells me he comes about four times a year. Sometimes with a friend or Missy but many times by himself. I find it odd at first, but he explains how it recharges him. The stress of our classes, finding a job, and behaving like the adults society expects can tear you apart, especially when you are fumbling along in the process of finding your way. I understand how a place that allows you to feel like a kid again can unite you with your inner child, and with no judgement from those around you since they are there for the same thing: an escape from reality.

"I hope you don't think I'm childish for this," he says, and I see how important my opinion is to him.

"I understand where you're coming from. Books are my escape from reality. Who's to say they are any more or less childish than coming here?" We're all looking for a reprieve from the stress that comes from adulthood.

He smiles. "Thanks."

Chewing my last bite, I glance between Mario and the floor of games. He pushes his empty plate away and leans back. "A place like this, casinos, video games, books... They're all distractions. Pick your poison, essentially. I don't think it's childish at all. If a person can't separate their alternate reality from the real one, that's not childish but rather a real problem. Thank you for sharing this with me. No one's ever thought to suggest a date like this."

His smile lights his face. "Are you ready to play then?"

I chuckle, and a blush warms my cheeks as my mind twists his words. "That's what she said."

Our refills arrive then. Mario grabs his glass and my free hand and pulls me from my stool. "Behave, princess!" he whispers in my ear. His breath teases the outer shell, goose bumps forming along my skin.

Aroused as hell, I grab his chin before he can straighten his body and rub my lips across them. A quick, firm kiss—no tongue and no teeth. By the time Mario reacts, I'm tugging him toward a machine.

"Oh my God! Pac-Man?"

He laughs. "You like it?"

"Hell yeah I like it. Let's play so I can kick your ass!"

CHAPTER 17

Mario's dates are hands down the best. He managed to kick my ass in Pac-Man but only after he insisted on best out of three. Poor sport couldn't handle the fact I beat him the first time. We flirted, laughed, and kissed our way across the large expanse of games. I can't remember ever having this much fun.

Playing with Mario reminds me of my childhood birthday parties. We even found two lanes of Skee-Ball. At one point, I shooed him off to play his zombie game while I perfected my throw.

We played until our credits ran out and then we walked the square and talked. He drove me home where we made out in the car for who knows how long before he walked me to my door.

Mario listens to what I say, he riles me up both sexually and mentally, and he's visually one of the hottest guys I have ever seen. My dates before him don't compare.

We talk every day and sneak in a visit here or there while at work. Sometimes I get to the breakroom early in the morning and find him waiting for me with my coffee in hand. One morning, I found a rose pinned under my windshield. Not one purchased in a store, the kind that grows in someone's garden.

He is nearly perfect. So what will happen? Am I really done with being Unlucky Izzy? No one is truly perfect, and I can't help but wonder if the other shoe will drop. Maybe he's another Zeke with a deal-breaking sexual glitch.

No way can I find another man who talks up his dick and then twitches throughout sex. Those would be some shitty odds. I think about it and groan. He must have a small dick. Or a bent dick. Maybe he's a mama's boy? Are these deal breakers?

"Earth to Izzy!" Jerry snaps.

"Sorry?"

"Don't you have a class to get to?" he asks.

I glance at the clock and jump up as I grab my bag. "Shit! Thanks, Jerry!" Hurrying out the office, I nearly topple over a few students passing at the same time. At the doors, I see Mario as he enters the building, and my body lights up like a Christmas tree. All the make-out sessions are catching up, and I'm an eager beaver. Or maybe my beaver is feeling eager?

"I thought you had class today?" he asks as I reach him.

After pressing my lips to his quickly, I force myself to back away. "I do. I'm late!" Spinning on my heels, I reach for the door and lose my balance. I correct myself to stop from hitting the ground only to bump into someone. "Oh! I'm so sorry!"

Angry green eyes snap to mine. "Watch where you're going, *skank!*"

At first, I'm in shock. Sure, I bumped into her, and it was careless of me, but I didn't think I'd committed such a grievous offense. She shoulder-checks me and snaps me out of my slight haze.

Looking past her, I see Mario. From his narrowed eyes, I know he watched the scene unfold. I'm late for class, and I can't exactly cause a scene in the building I work. He says something to her before he hurries toward me.

"You okay, princess?" he asks, and his hand cups my cheek.

I look past him and find her staring daggers at us. "I'm fine. Exes, huh?"

"Yeah, sorry about that," he whispers.

I nod and take a step back. "I really need to get to class."

"Hurry!" he says, and I rush out the door, this time avoiding any exes lurking around the corner.

A variety of emotions go through me while I run down the sidewalk. My backpack bounces off my back as I push off one foot and then the other. Other students barely give me a second glance as I rush past them, nearing the building. Most days, I see a dozen individuals doing a mad dash like I am today. I slip inside the classroom and find a seat in the back, and sweat rolls down my spine. I find my water bottle and take a deep pull as I push aside the scene with Mario and his ex and listen to the professor.

Before I know it, I'm packing up my things. Unlike my arrival, I take my time leaving. I've finished my hours at the library for the day and have no other reason to stay on campus. I briefly consider finding Mario, but the last thing I want is drama.

My phone vibrates, and it's as though I've conjured him.

Mario: How was class?
Izzy: Boring.
Mario: Heading home?

Izzy: Yup.

I wait a little, but he doesn't send me another message. It's probably for the best. The scene earlier reminded me too much of high school. I'm nearly done with college. I didn't like that shit in high school, let alone now when I expect others to behave like the adults their driver's licenses claim they are.

After pulling my keys from my pocket, I press the lock button twice. As much as I'm on campus, I can never find my car. I hear it beep, and I weave through another row of cars toward it. My memory kicks in, and I go right to where I parked.

"Hi, princess!" Mario greets me with a smile and two cups.

"Hi. What are you doing here?" I ask, genuinely happy and surprised to see him leaning against my door.

He sets both cups on my car before his hands cup my face, and his lips brush against mine, soft and warm. His tongue glides along the seam of my mouth, and I open for him. The kiss is sweet at first, then it turns hungry.

When he presses his forehead against mine, I realize my back is to my car. Our breaths are fast pants as we regain our composure. I whimper at the feel of his erection pressing against me. One kiss from Mario and I'm mush. After Dave & Buster's, I tried convincing myself it would be smart to wait on taking this to the next level, but after these intense moments, I don't know if I can.

Mario has left the ball in my court, and I'm ready to do something about it. Maybe not all of it but fuck if I'll go much longer without seeing what he's packing.

"It's hard to think when you're looking at me like that," he whispers, his voice deep and gravelly.

I press my thighs together and shrug. "You started it."

He brushes his lips against mine, a faint kiss before he moves to my ear. "You make me forget where we are."

The front of my body cools when he steps back and hands me a cup. "Hot chocolate?"

"Thanks. Are you trying to smooth-talk me?"

"Nah, it's a peace offering. I'm really sorry for how Missy treated you earlier. It wasn't cool at all."

I study his face and see he's still angry about it. "No, it wasn't." I take a sip of my steaming beverage and let the creamy chocolate relax me. "What bug crawled up her ass?"

Mario sighs and leans against my car. "I think she saw us kiss and is jealous."

"Ah," I mutter and sip some more. "So, to what do I owe this nice surprise?"

"I was hoping we could hang out tonight?" he says, a sweet smile tipping his lips.

I tap my finger on my chin. "Well, you did bring me chocolate, and you did call out Missy immediately after the shit she pulled. I think that all qualifies for a treat." My mind dips straight into dirty, sexy images of treats. Before I know it, I'm crossing my ankles and clamping down on the heat building between my thighs.

Mario pins me against my car. His forearms lean against it at each side of my head. His eyes are dark with desire, and I bet he sees the same thing reflecting from mine.

He presses himself against me. "I've got a treat for you all right."

I chuckle, but it sounds breathless. "You're so cheesy sometimes."

"It may be true, but it doesn't turn you off." His eyes move between us. "You're turned on as hell right now."

I don't deny the truth. If he presses his thigh against

my sex, it wouldn't take much for me to come. Just a little friction. I'm wound tight, and I know I told myself another week, but what does it matter at this point? Mario has stopped us every single time from doing more than I'm ready for. Staring into his aroused eyes, I know neither of us will be pulling the rip cord. We can't deny ourselves this passion any longer.

"I'll meet you at your place. I'm going to swing by mine and then I'll bring us some dinner. Text me what you want," he says and then his mouth is on mine, devouring me with each lick and swipe of his tongue. I wrap my arms around his neck carefully as he presses me into the car.

Nearly crazy with the need to have him fill me, I forget where we are. He bites down on my lip, not hard enough to draw blood but enough to get my attention. He leans his head against my collarbone, and I close my eyes. Our breaths sound ragged from the sparks of desire driving us rabid.

"Get in the car," he nearly growls.

I press my lips to his for a quick peck and slip out from my cage. Mario steps back when I pull on the door handle and grabs the door frame. After I'm settled, I blow him a kiss, and he shuts the door. With a wave, I leave him behind, my mind thinking of all the ways I plan to explore the body I've been dreaming about.

We haven't sexted or gone past heavy petting in these weeks together. I know it's absurd, considering my past adventures. But like I said, Mario has kept us both in control from rushing things. I've touched the firm planes under his shirt, but I've yet to see or taste them. A steady hum flows over my body. This *need* is raw and powerful.

Is this what it feels like to be a sex-deprived sex addict?

CHAPTER 18

My skin is smooth. There isn't an unwanted hair left on my body, and I've lathered it with lotion, taking extra care to avoid my nipples and neck. Who wants to taste lotion? Ew! The shower spray had been excruciating on my aching nipples, but I didn't allow myself to ease the throbbing of my clit.

Not wanting to look like I'd been running around preening myself, I chose a cute but relaxed outfit: skeleton leggings with a loose tank and no jewelry except a pair of stud earrings and my watch.

I check my phone and realize I haven't warned Val to stay away. Realizing my mistake, I shoot her a quick text. She reminds me of her plans to stay with Mason at his place. Wringing my hands, I look around the room, unsure if I should light a candle or sit and relax with an episode of *Hawaii 5-0* on Netflix.

A knock on the door resolves my internal debate. Once I see Mario through the peep hole, butterflies take off in my stomach. With a deep breath, I attempt to calm my nerves. It's Mario. It's not the first time he's come over to hang out. He's done everything right so far.

Knock. Knock. Knock.

I turn the knob, pull the door open, and smile. His hair is damp and finger-combed back. I smell his cologne and—from the logo on the bag in his hand—chimichangas. A delicious combination. Man and food. No man should discount that the way into a woman's heart is through damn good food too.

"What's that smile for?" he asks and rubs his lips against mine.

"I was just thinking about the phrase 'the way to a man's heart is through food.' Whoever came up with it didn't realize the same could be said for women."

He chuckles as he kicks off his shoes. "Well, I know how much you love their chimichangas, and you never did text me to say what you wanted." Mario places the bag on the counter and pulls me into him. He cradles my face and gives me a proper kiss, my toes curling in response. "There, much better..." he says against my lips.

My eyes flutter open, and my stomach growls loudly as the smell reminds me I'm starving for more than just Mario.

"I better get this food in you before you pass out," he jokes and releases me.

We talk while we eat, laughing and sharing stories from our childhood. Talking to Mario is easy and natural. I've told him things I never wanted to with Zeke or Johnny. In return, I've learned new things about Mario. Any question I ask, no matter the topic, he answers.

Once we finish, we throw out the trash and curl up on the couch.

"What do you want to watch?" I ask. He takes the control and picks a comedy neither of us have seen.

We relax together as our food settles. His fingers run up and down the side of my arm in a pattern, leaving goose bumps along my flesh. As the movie goes on, we realize it's a bust. Halfway through it, I turn it off without a word, unable to take more of the bad acting, and straddle his thighs. My palms press against his pecs, and I smile when they twitch under my touch.

His hands move to my waist. His thumbs slip under the fabric, finding skin, and I notice his eyes move toward the door. "Is Val hanging out with Mason tonight?"

I can't help but smile. "Mmhmm..."

"So we have the apartment all to ourselves tonight?"

"Yup!"

He nods slowly. Neither of us move, with the exception of his thumbs as they tease the hell out of me. A moment passes before our mouths clash and our lips press together. Our teeth clink, and we chuckle. Tongues glide along each other, and I'm moaning into his mouth.

Mario's kisses are seriously the best I've had. When our tongues meet, an electric current runs through my body and my nipples perk up, begging for attention. I move my hand to his face, his five-o'clock shadow rough against my palm. He normally keeps his face shaven and smooth. I assume he skipped shaving it in his haste to come over.

My fingers run through his short hair, thick silky strands at the top before it shortens on the way to his neck. Tipping my head to the side, I deepen our kiss. There's no slobber or stabbing pointed-tongue action. His moves are practiced and sexy, and I can't help but imagine how good it will be between us.

Mario pulls back, and his eyes are wild and out of control. He looks sexier than ever, and I long to see him naked. He grabs the hem to my tank, and I raise my arms above my head so he can pull it off. His eyes move to my chest, the tops of my breasts jiggling when I lower my arms. A groan of appreciation slips from his lips, and I chuckle.

"What?" he asks.

"No one's ever groaned from seeing me in a bra," I say and tug at his shirt.

He reaches behind him and pulls it off. "And no one else will ever see you in a bra again."

I hear his words, but I'm busy staring at his chest. All the times I caressed him over his clothes, I knew he hid a toned body. Seeing it made me realize I was wrong. He is cut. Divots and firm muscles sculpt his upper torso.

"Now who's groaning?" he teases.

"Why haven't we made out without our shirts again?" I ask as I lean forward to kiss the soft tan skin in front of me.

Mario gasps when my lips brush against his skin. "Because we were trying to not rush things, and I knew one look at what was hidden under them would be the end of me." His mouth presses hot kisses against my neck and down over the tops of my breasts.

My hips move on their own, squirming against his lap at the sensations swarming my body. The rough pads of his fingers glide up my back, and the cups to my bra sag. He pushes me back, and I suck in a breath as the straps slip down my arms until I'm bare to him.

"Fuck, princess," he mutters, and his thumbs barely rub against the pointed peaks. "I've never…"

Mario swallows his words and then his mouth is covering one nipple and massaging my other breast. My head falls back as I hold his head to me. His tongue flicks the tip, and his teeth lightly saws over it before taking a big pull.

If I thought my clit was throbbing earlier, I was mistaken. "Mario, please," I beg.

He switches breasts and repeats the same sweet torture on the other one. My breath is coming in erratic puffs that have no rhyme or reason. I've never experienced so much pleasure at a man playing with my breasts. The mix of tongue, teeth, pinching, and massaging has me losing my mind.

He releases my breast with a pop and licks his full lips as his eyes meet mine. Mario cups my ass and stands. I yelp in surprise and lock my hands and ankles around him. My breasts press against his warm, bare skin. Peppering my neck with kisses, he walks us down the hall. We've hung out in my bedroom before, so he knows where to go. He kicks the door shut with his foot and helps me to my feet at the side of my bed.

His hands make quick work of undoing my jeans and pulling them down my body. Standing in only a thong, I force my hands to hang loosely at my sides. His gaze is like a caress as he takes his fill of my nearly naked form. My thumbs slip under the tiny lace to pull them down, but his hands stop me.

"Not yet. We'll get there. I promise. Get on the bed."

After tossing the covers to the side, I crawl in backward onto the center of the bed and lean on my elbows. "You're still overdressed," I say. My voice sounds sultry and unlike my own.

Mario undoes his belt and button and lowers the zipper some. His pants peek open a sliver, and I don't see any fabric behind the denim. My legs quiver, and my core tightens.

"Now you're teasing me." I whimper and bite my lip.

He chuckles. "Are you sure you're ready to do this? We can go back out there and watch TV while we cuddle."

"Shut the fuck up and get naked. I'm dying over here."

Mario chuckles. "Such a dirty mouth on you."

My eyes flick downward. "By the bulge struggling to

free itself, you like my dirty mouth."

When he pushes his jeans down, his dick springs up. It's hard, long, and thick. My mouth waters with the need to run my tongue over the veins I see and the broad head glistening with one single drop at the tip.

To answer my question, he's packing. Not some monster you only see in pornos or hear about in romance novels. The kind you imagine filling you completely. Stretching you but not to the point of pain.

His dick bounces a little, and my eyes meet Mario's. I expect him to make some corny comment like "like what you see," but it never comes. Instead, he grabs a strip of condoms from his discarded jeans and tosses it on the nightstand.

The bed shifts when he climbs on it and settles at my side. He takes his time caressing me. I shift, and my back arches under his touch. I'm losing my mind, but I don't want to rush our first time. He's exceeding all my prior lovers, and we haven't had any form of sex yet.

I'm not sure how much time goes by. Our hands have been running along each other as we memorize every inch of skin. We kiss, but they aren't out of control, just sweet presses of lips and tongue unlike the passionate devouring from earlier.

"Please, Mario," I beg. I can't take more of this sweet torture. My clit hurts, and my internal muscles won't stop clenching, needing something to wrap around.

His fingers tweak my nipple hard, and I groan. "I've got you, princess." His hand slips under the band to my thong. One long finger finds my opening and presses inside. My back bows at the pleasure, and my mouth falls open on a gasp. His finger slips out and rubs slow circles on my clit, and the heat in my belly coils tight.

Opening my eyes, I find him watching me, his eyes dilated with pleasure. His finger slows, and I whimper.

"So close, baby."

A slow, sexy smile lights his face. "You look absolutely gorgeous right now, flushed with the need to come. The sounds you're making... God, I don't know how I got so lucky." Two fingers slip into me and curl against my G-spot. One leg falls to the bed, and the other against Mario. His dick presses against my side, and I need to touch it, to feel his hot skin. As my hand reaches for him, Mario removes his hand. My eyes snap to his with confusion.

"If you touch me, this is going to be all over," he says and kneels between my legs. Mario removes my thong and tosses it aside. His hands run up my legs until his thumbs meet the apex between my thighs. He teases the hell out of me by touching the edge of my sex. "Such a pretty pussy. Are you ready for me to taste it?"

I whimper at his dirty words and nod. His finger moves down my sex before he pushes it in, then brings it to his lips. Mario moans around his index and lowers himself.

His tongue slides up my center and flicks my bundle of nerves. "I want your eyes on me," he demands. I nod and then his mouth is on me.

Holy shitballs. I can't explain it even if I tried. Mario's mouth is pure magic. Maybe it's because he's wound me up for so many hours? Maybe he's had a lot of practice—nope, I refuse to accept this one. Maybe his tongue is a pussy whisperer?

Within a minute, I come long and hard. When my spasms slow, he presses two fingers inside and draws another orgasm from me. This one is shorter, but the intensity causes my toes to curl and my hips to buck against his mouth.

"Wow." I pant and notice his proud smile.

"Good?" he asks before fastening his mouth back

onto my sex.

I nod. My body twitches, the flicks over my sensitive bud almost painful. "Ah! Baby, too much."

He wipes his mouth with the back of his hands after licking his fingers clean. "Seeing you come is my new favorite activity."

I laugh. "You're very talented at it." Looking between us, I see his hard and almost angry-looking erection reaching for me. "Now, I need *you* inside me."

Mario rips a condom off the strip he brought and offers it to me. Using my teeth, I pry it open and dump the condom onto my palm. After a second of fumbling, I sit up and reach for him but stop.

"Wha—"

My lips wrap around his engorged tip, answering his cut-off question.

He's warm and smooth and too big to comfortably deep-throat. His fingers delve into my hair as a moan vibrates through him. I pull him out slowly, making sure to hold the suction around him, swirling my tongue around the tip before flicking it along the nerves just below the head.

"Fuck," he groans before gently pushing me away.

I chuckle and slip the condom down his length. Meeting his eyes, I see his control is slipping. In that moment, I feel powerful knowing I'm making him as crazed as I feel.

CHAPTER 19

"Lay back."

He covers me with his body, his firm muscles complementing my softness. Mario's kisses contradict our rabid need. He's slow, without a rush in the world, emotions flowing between us with only the touch of our lips and tongue.

He presses the tip of his erection against my entrance, and I moan into his mouth. I want him—no, I need him like I need air.

Why is this different than the others?

Each touch, kiss, and caress with Mario is deeper and more intimate than the act of sex with any other person. In the back of my mind, I know I should be scared, but all I can drum up is excitement.

After months of dating in the hope of finding someone I click with, I've met and kissed an army of frogs. I watched Mario from afar, never thinking he felt anything toward me past polite indifference. And now here I am, my legs shaking and goose bumps covering me as Mario pushes his thickness into me.

I gasp. All thoughts flit away as he fills me inch by

glorious inch. Our kiss turns desperate and wild as he pulls his hips away and slides back in. Locking my ankles around his waist, I meet each of his thrusts. My breaths are ragged, and I break the kiss. Pushing my face into his shoulder, I focus solely on the sensations of our union.

Mario is all around me, his scent, his breaths, his warmth. My insides clench around him, and my body tightens. His hand slips between us, and the moment his fingers pluck at my clit, my back arches off the mattress. Mario's thrusts come faster and harder, and my lips part in a silent cry.

I dig my nails into his shoulders and hold on. The flashes of light behind my eyes begin to disappear, and I try to catch my breath from the climax. The muscles under my fingers tense, and I run my tongue up the tendons in his neck as he chases his own release.

"Come, baby, come…" I whisper between breaths. A few more thrusts and his hips push against me, and he buries his face in my neck.

When he lifts his head, I see beads of sweat along his brow. There's a softness to his eyes I've never seen before. My chest tightens in response to it, and I swallow past a lump in my throat.

Mario watches me a moment and lowers his mouth to mine. This kiss is emotional and tender, and it presses buttons I never realized I had. He pulls back and smiles. It's relaxed and satisfied in a way I haven't seen.

"Hi," I whisper, unsure what else to say or do.

He leans his weight onto one arm and brushes my hair from my face. "Hi, princess." His thumb strokes my cheek as my hands run lazy patterns along his back. "I better go clean up," he says and presses his lips to my forehead.

Tears prickle the backs of my eyes. There is something about a kiss on your forehead from a man you care about that is so powerful and dangerous to your heart. Luckily, he doesn't notice, and we both sigh at his withdrawal. I follow him with my eyes as he walks away, studying his firm ass cheeks with their divots from his workouts. Hot damn, he's got a fine ass. I imagine biting the round flesh, and heat fills my belly.

Three orgasms. This man has satisfied me, and here I am gearing up for another. Before tonight, I was lucky if I could get two releases with a man in a night. I obviously suck at dating, and I wasn't much better at finding generous lovers.

Mario returns, and I raise to my elbows, drinking in every bit of him—broad shoulders with firm muscles, a nice six-pack, muscular thighs, and his dick. Even in its now-flaccid state, it's a sight to behold. He's a shower not a grower.

He slips into my bed, grabs the covers, and gathers me into his arms. "That was better than all my fantasies combined."

Looking up, I smile. "Oh, yeah?"

He cups my face. "Izzy—" Mario sighs, and his eyes bounce from my eyes to my mouth a few times. "I wouldn't lie to you. I hope you realize that by now."

"I know."

"Princess, you mean a lot to me," he whispers against my lips before kissing me, a sweet, tender expression of emotion.

I lay my head on his chest and close my eyes. It doesn't take long before I fall into a deep, restful sleep. When I wake hours later, I'm on my right side with Mario wrapped around me. Our fingers are linked and lie between my breasts. His soft breaths blow tendrils of hair along my neck, and his dick is hard and tucked between our bodies.

There is something so intimate in our position. I've

never woken in a man's arms. I relive each touch and kiss between us from last night and smile. My chest squeezes, and I realize this emotion is new to me. I'm falling for this man. Maybe I've already landed on my head.

Mario has checked off all the imaginary boxes of what I want in a man. He's funny, kind, caring, considerate, and hot damn, the sex is off the charts. I'm not stupid. We haven't been together very long, but how I feel is solid.

Before my mind can spiral out of control, he squeezes my hand. "G'morning, princess."

I squirm against him, my heart racing in my chest. "Hi."

He releases my hand, and his fingers run along my belly. "How'd you sleep?"

Best sleep ever! "I slept well, you?"

Mario nuzzles my neck, and a shiver runs over me. "Great. Best night's sleep I can remember in a long time. I think I have you to thank for it." His lips leave a trail of hot sexual heat, and my ass wiggles against him. He chuckles and presses his hips forward.

I reach behind me and explore the muscles of his hip and ass, something I wanted to do last night but never got the chance to. Mario's hands are teasing one nipple and running up and down my leg before disappearing between my thighs.

There's no rush, but each touch is lighting me up, and I'm ready to be filled by him. With his lazy swirls and pinches, he draws out an orgasm. I arch against him and gasp with pleasure and surprise at the climax.

When my muscles loosen, his hand slips free, and he reaches for a condom. I start to turn onto my back, but he stops me. "Stay like this."

I hear the foil tear, and a few seconds later, he's prodding my entrance. He's deeper in this position, thoroughly filling me. I press my head back against his chest, and his arms encircle me from behind. One hand caresses and plays with my breasts, and the other strums my bud of nerves. His thigh and ass flexes under my palm, and I explore whatever I can reach.

My climax in this position is different. From deep within, I coil until pleasure bursts through the seams holding me together. I contract around him, and a moan rips free. The sound of our flesh meeting and our short pants reach my ears.

Mario's hands don't cease their attention as he shifts his angle. With each stroke, he presses a sweet spot that sends my heart racing. His hips piston himself in and out, leaving me unable to fully absorb the tremors of my orgasm before another hits.

"Fuck," he groans, the puff of air tickling my neck as I break into a million pieces.

His fingers go gentle on my sensitized skin, and his lips descend on my neck. The tender kisses sooth me as we float back from our shared ecstasy. Mario's heart thunders against my back, and joy fills my heart. He's as affected by our union as I am.

Before I can begin to contemplate the other emotions swirling around, we groan in unison as Mario pulls each glorious inch out of me. I roll onto my back and stare at the ceiling while he discards the condom in my bathroom.

"Come on, princess."

Accepting his hand, I ask, "What's up?"

"Let's go shower."

Mario—wet, slick, and my hands all over those firm muscles? No woman would even question it, no matter how weak her legs are after coming.

Showering with Mario goes differently than I imagined—probably because both of us are rather sated and experiencing a post-orgasm bliss. His fingers are divine against my scalp, tiny sparks soothing each hair follicle he massages. After washing and rinsing my hair, he lathers my loofah.

How many times had he done this to Missy? I bite my cheek and shove the thought aside. Missy doesn't belong anywhere around us.

Once every inch of me is rinsed, I give him the same treatment. Leaving the best part for last, my soapy hands make sure his heavy balls and dick are free of come.

He twitches and thickens in my hand. "Princess," Mario warns as his fingers encircle my wrist. His eyes light up when he chuckles at my pout.

"Oh, fine, you're no fun."

Mario cups my face and kisses me after shutting off the water. "We can break in your shower next time."

Next time. Logically I know we are in a relationship, and now that we've uncapped the genie, there is no putting him back. Hearing Mario's reminder of more to come sends the butterflies in my belly into flight.

Mario grabs a towel and dries me off gently before wrapping it around me. I rise to my toes. "Thanks," I whisper and kiss him.

"Jesus, it smells like sweaty sex in here," Val says, startling us both.

Mario turns toward the door, and we stand side by side. Neither of us miss the way her eyes bulge when they move over his body and linger a second longer over his semi-hard dick hanging between his legs.

"Oh my God!" she cries as Mario moves behind me. "I'm so—sorry, I didn't—I'll be in the kitchen!" Her words come quickly, and she runs out of my room.

Mario chuckles behind me. "That wasn't awkward at all."

I cover my mouth with my hand and shake my head. "Not at all… I'm never going to hear the end of this."

He pulls my back to his front and wraps his arms around my belly, his head in the crook of my neck.

"The fact she saw you naked..."

His head moves against my shoulder in what I think is a nod. "And she hasn't seen a dick before? I mean, I thought she and Mason were... you know." There's a teasing tone to his words, and I giggle.

"Of course, she's seen one, and yes those two are definitely having sex—"

"I guess I don't see the problem. I mean, other than she saw her best friend's boyfriend's dick," he says and turns me, my towel falling to the floor in the process. His hands cup my hips, and my nipples graze his chest.

I lay my arms on him, my fingers caressing the tops of his shoulders. "Baby, the problem is based on the expression on her face, she's never going to let it go. You aren't exactly an average-size man."

"I'm not?" he teases.

I laugh. "Do you need me to praise the size of your dick?"

Oh, Lord, please don't say you do.

"No, but I really like hearing your thoughts on the matter." He punctuates his words by pressing his hardness against me. My breath quickens, and I want him again. His hand snakes between us and finds my entrance. "Damn, princess. You're wet for me?" At his touch, I bite my lip and whimper. "How about you tell me what you think about my dick?"

The dirty talk sends more heat flooding to my sex. "It's the nicest one to pleasure me," I whisper, my cheeks flushing at the words.

Mario slides two fingers into me. "What makes it so nice?" he mutters against my ear, and a shudder rocks my body.

"The way it fills me. Just when I think I can't take

any more, you surprise me by going balls deep." My breaths turn into little pants at his touch and the words I've spoken aloud.

Mario growls and nips my neck. "Come on." He grabs my arm and guides me to the bed. "On your hands and knees."

I hear another condom wrapper rip, and a moment later, he's pressing at my entrance. His hand gently pushes my shoulders to the bed, my ass in the air as his other hand caresses it. Mario thrusts into me in one fluid motion, filling me completely, his balls slapping against me. I gasp at this new angle. If I thought he'd filled me before, I was wrong.

We groan in unison, but before I can even begin to adjust, his fingers dig into my hips. There's no foreplay. No teasing thrusts to build the pleasure between us. We're lost as he possesses me with each stroke, pounding into me. All his control is gone while he marks me as his. There are no words for the emotions swelling in my heart. His touch is firm and yet gentle. One word from me and I know he will stop. But why?

Our moans fill the room, and it doesn't take long before my body tenses, my back arches, and pure ecstasy overcomes me. My muscles spasm around him and he grunts, pushing into me harder before we collapse in a heap.

Mario's heavy, but he's not crushing me. Our hearts slow, and he trails kisses over my back as he begins to rise. The sweet affection wraps around my heart and squeezes my life force.

"Holy shit." I pant, needing to focus on the physical joy and not the scary strong emotions swirling around my heart.

"I didn't hurt you, did I?" He presses one last kiss between my shoulder blades and slips free.

I gasp as the movement causes my body to twitch. "Uh-uh," I mutter and roll to my side to watch him. He disposes of the condom and lies down. Curling into him, I drape my leg over his and relax. "You're so comfy."

Mario kisses my head and chuckles. "I'm glad. I love having you in my arms like this."

"Mmmm…"

"Izzy?"

"Mhmm…"

"I'm sure Val and the neighbors heard us that time," he says carefully.

Thinking over his words for a second, I realize I'm too sated and tired to care. That was some of the best sex in my life. I've been subjected to Mason and Val's sexcapades. The woman can handle one from me.

CHAPTER 20

When I think of all the crappy dates I've been on, I cringe. Don't get me wrong, I've learned a lot about myself during this process: what I want and don't want, deal breakers, and a wonderful reminder that crappy humans do exist.

Mario isn't perfect, but his imperfections call to my own. We are in tune, always surprising each other when we meet up after a long day with the same thing on our minds. On one occasion, we both bought Mexican food without telling the other we were picking up dinner. After an overfilled stomach, we promised to share in advance if we planned on grabbing dinner in the future.

Even with Zeke, whom outside of sex I got along with well, I didn't experience this connection. Now that Mario and I have had sex—a trivial word for what we shared—the edginess which followed us around has disappeared.

Mario is generous, kind, funny, and smart. These last few weeks, he's shown me with his actions, words, and through his touch that this thing between us isn't one-sided. All those crappy dates before him had taken a bat to my hope in finding a decent and caring man.

I'm scared. Is it possible my nasty streak of awful men is over?

Don't punish Mario for the other men you dated, Val advised me last night when she found me worrying my hands.

She's not wrong. It would be unfair to Mario to punish and expect him to do what the others did. He's done nothing but the right thing, and my gut feeling is singing happiness.

When will the other shoe drop? Am I so used to the bad that I'll ruin this, self-sabotaging us before we can flourish into something beautiful?

"Hi, princess!" The velvety sound pushes away the ominous cloud I've allowed to form over me. His smile brightens his face, and I calm at his presence when he enters the copy office. I'm filled with happiness as butterflies flap around inside my stomach, a welcome dance Mario cannot see.

"Hi!" I push to my feet and move to the counter. We lean over the obstacle and kiss, a sweet brush of our lips.

His brow furrows, his eyes filling with concern. "Are you okay? You seemed miles away just now."

I lean my elbows on the counter and bite my lip. The anxiety from before trickles back in. "Yeah, I was just thinking."

He puts his bag down at his feet and mirrors my position. "About what?"

"You. Me... Us," I whisper, unable to meet his eyes. I know I should keep my worries to myself, but I'm incapable of holding my thoughts and emotions from this man.

He nods slowly. "Can you elaborate before I start thinking the worst?"

I inhale through my nose and rub my hands over my

face, thankful I didn't put on any makeup this morning. "I guess I'm just a bit nervous about it all. I haven't exactly had a great track record."

"I see," he mutters, but before he can say more, a few students enter and cross to the supplies at the table. Mario takes my hand in his and studies my face while we wait for another moment of privacy. He runs his thumb over my skin in circles, the small movements calming me.

"Hey, girl!" Val says excitedly, and her eyes shift to Mario. "Hey, stud!"

"Hey," we reply in unison before sharing a knowing smile.

"Are you joining us for food?" she asks Mario as the group leaves the office.

"No, I won't intrude on your time." He squeezes my hand in his. "Are you up for dinner tonight, and we can continue our talk?"

I study his face and see the shadow of worry he now carries. My hand cups his cheek, and I lean forward to place my lips on his warm ones. I infuse as much comfort and emotion into the kiss as I can without allowing it to become too heated.

"I'll be at Mason's tonight, so you two can scandalize the building without traumatizing me." Val snickers, and I can see her cheesy grin from the corner of my eye.

"Pick me up at six?"

He nods. "Bye, princess." He winks and grabs his bag. "Bye, Val."

Watching him as he leaves, I note the slump in his shoulders, and my heart squeezes tight. I did that. He was happy to see me, but I put that look on his face.

"Oh, honey, what's the matter?" Val asks.

"I think I've just ruined this," I say, pointing toward

the empty doorway.

"I seriously doubt that. Mario adores you. He did seem a little sad when he left, but the sparks between you are shining bright."

After telling her about the short conversation Mario and I exchanged before she and the students came in, she wraps her arms around me. "Oh, Izzy, silly girl. Being afraid and worried is normal. You need to talk to him about it, now that you've left him hanging like that. Poor guy is going to worry all day until tonight."

I sigh. She's right, and I know if I were in his shoes, I would lose my mind. After hugging her tight, I step back and grab my phone.

Izzy: I'm looking forward to seeing you tonight. I'm sorry we couldn't talk now.

Mario: Me too.

Mario: Can you at least tell me if you still want to be with me?

Tears prick the backs of my eyes at his last text. My heart pounds, and emotion clogs my throat.

Izzy: Yes!

Mario: Okay, then we can figure out the rest tonight. Go enjoy your time with Val.

My nerves ease at his words, and I tuck the phone into my back pocket. "Ready to go?"

Val nods. "Is everything better?"

I shrug. "I hate that I've made him worry."

Val narrows her eyes and breathes in deeply. Her thoughts seem loud, but she only stares at me.

"What?"

"You love him," she whispers.

I freeze and listen to her words on repeat in my head. Fear crawls up my spine, and goose bumps form across my flesh. "I... I—"

Val helps me into my seat. "Are you okay? Breathe!"

Sucking in air at her words, I meet her eyes. "No, it's too soon. It's too soon, right? Is it possible to fall in love in this short time? No, it's just lust—"

"Whoa! Calm down, honey. I don't know if it's too soon or not, but I do think you need to reflect on how you really feel. How about we put a lid on this and get some food? I don't think you're ready to talk about it now, and I'm sorry for suggesting it."

I nod slowly and let her help me up after a moment of thought. Lunch goes quickly, and Val spends it talking about Mason and her classes. Her kind eyes watch me as I respond as needed.

Do I love him? The words play on a loop in the back of my mind. If I thought I was scared before, this has pushed me straight into absolutely terrified.

"Izzy?" Val says with a wave of her hand.

"Sorry?"

"I'm really sorry I made you freak out even more. If it matters… I wouldn't be surprised if Mario feels… strongly for you too."

The rest of my day goes by in a blur. My focus is shot, and my replies to students and Jerry are short. I can't help but play a variety of scenarios of how things will go with Mario in my mind. Scattered into those same thoughts, I analyze my feelings.

Is Val right? Am I in love with Mario? Or is this simply lust?

If I accept the first, will I find myself holding the remaining shards of my heart when it's all over? Do I even deserve a man like Mario?

After a few hours of my erratic emotional state, Jerry sends me home early. I take an extra-long, hot shower and crawl into bed. When I wake from my nap, I'm calmer but realize I'm now running late for my date. I dress quickly, throwing on a pair of skinny jeans and a pretty violet blouse. The actions force my mind to ignore my nerves for our upcoming conversation, even if only for a little time.

The moment I hear the knock, I freeze, my glass of water partly tipped toward my lips. My pulse speeds, and I feel each throb of the valve in my heart as blood rushes through it. After a cleansing breath, I place the glass in the sink and go to the door. Peering out, I see Mario cup the back of his neck. His eyes are cast downward, and my heart clenches. I can almost feel the worry coming off him in waves through the door. My own insecurities have upset him, and I wish I would have been more careful.

When I open the door, I smile. "Hi, baby!"

His eyes meet mine, and a flash of relief soothes some of the lines creasing his forehead. "Hi, princess."

He steps into me, and I sigh when he brushes his lips over mine. My arms slide over his abs and wrap around his middle until I grab handfuls of fabric at his back. I don't want to let go. I'm not sure what it is about this man, but the simple act of hugging calms the restlessness I've been experiencing.

Mario tucks me into his side and guides us into the apartment. "I hope you don't mind, but I'd prefer uninterrupted privacy for our conversation from earlier?"

I nod my head against his chest and look up at him. He studies my face a moment before kissing my forehead. I close my eyes at the sensation, drawing in the emotion that washes over me. "Do you want something to drink first?" I whisper.

He chuckles. "I don't think the knots in my stomach can handle anything."

"I'm sorry," I mutter, a boulder landing at the bottom of my stomach. My words did this to him. It's not as if he's done anything wrong. If anything, he's done everything right, and I don't know how to handle it. Do I handle it? Is there anything to "handle"?

Mario squeezes me tightly before walking us the last few feet to the couch, and we sit. We turn toward each other, our shins pressing against each other's. He takes my hand into his warm one. His thumbs run small comforting circles over my skin, and I think about where I should start—or continue, in this case.

He clears his throat and meets my eyes. "Have I told you that Missy was my only serious girlfriend?"

I shake my head. Unsure where he's going, I remain quiet, curious about why he's mentioning *her*.

"I dated a few girls, but nothing clicked with them. Things with Missy... Well, at first we were only friends. I cared about her, and it grew into love." His eyes shift behind me, clearly uncomfortable with the topic. "Things between us were... *different*. There was no instant burn or yearning. I respected and cared for her deeply, but then things changed." Mario's smile doesn't quite reach his eyes. "One glance in your direction, and I found myself *needing* to steal just one more look. The guilt I felt was awful. Not because I'd done anything wrong, but because I realized I felt more for a complete stranger than the woman I claimed to love."

"Mario—"

"Please let me finish," he pleads.

I nod. "I'm sorry, please continue."

"I know it's not cool to mention my ex. I know our relationship is new. I know *this*"—he waves his hand between us—"is terrifying for you... Izzy, I'm sorry you met some idiots before me, but I'm not sorry it happened. I haven't been this happy in a long time—or ever. I like where this is going and how I feel when I'm with you. I hope you don't let your fears mess up this great thing between us."

Mario's words fly from his mouth a mile a minute,

but I didn't miss one word. My heart is racing, and I'm filled with utter joy. He's not wrong at all. Maybe I am falling in love with him, or it's possible I've already fallen. It doesn't matter.

"Oh, so now you're going to stay quiet?" He teases, but his eyes are shadowed by his own fears.

My smile pulls my face back tight, and I climb onto his lap. I cradle his face with my hands and stare into his eyes before I capture his lips. I infuse our kiss with all the emotion coursing through me. His fingers dig into my hips, and his prodding erection pushes onto my center. This isn't about sex. No, this is so much more. Don't get me wrong; I want this man with every fiber of my being.

I force myself to pull back. My chest rises and falls quickly, and I'm sure he doesn't miss the movement, but his eyes stay on mine. Waiting. It's my turn, and as I consider what put me in such a terrified funk earlier, I realize how silly I've been acting.

"I obviously haven't had luck with men. To be honest, I don't think I deserve you. I *am* terrified, but it hurts me when I try to imagine my life without you in it. We click. It almost scares me at how well we understand each other. We haven't been together long, and if I feel this strongly now... I'll be devastated if this doesn't work out."

Mario's mouth opens, but I press my finger across his lips.

"Uh-uh. My turn, mister!" I smirk, and he nods, his eyes crinkled with amusement. "Earlier I was having this momentary freak-out and then you walked in and saw right through me. That frightened me even more. I really do like where this is going, and I can't promise you I won't freak out again. And for the record, I'm not sorry you weren't in love with Missy. You are who you are because of the man you became thanks to the time with her. Talking about her doesn't bother me. She's your past, and I hope you see me as your future. I'm sorry I worried you."

I lower my finger from his lips and kiss them again. His hand cups my cheek, and I nuzzle it.

"You done?" he whispers.

"Mhmm…" I mutter, relieved to get my fears off my chest. This wasn't a declaration of love, but it's clear to me we are headed in that direction.

"Are you sure? I want to make sure we close the chapter on this freak-out."

Closing my eyes, I think for a moment. I can feel Mario's gaze as he watches me evaluate my emotions. "No, I'm good now. A bump in the road as I wondered if the other shoe would drop."

"I'm glad to hear that. For the record, you weren't the only one worried about heartache. Now, let's go get dinner before I lose my last bit of control." He says the latter as he grinds his hips up into me.

Warmth spreads in my belly at the contact, and I bite my lower lip. This man can make me forget my name. Heat floods my body, and I roll my hips on him, looking for the friction only he can give. Dinner can wait. I need to make sure Mario knows I'm in this with him.

CHAPTER 21

I'm freezing. It doesn't matter I'm wearing Mario's sweatshirt. A few hours in this library and I'm an icicle. After telling Circulation I'll be back in ten, I head outside to bask in the warm sun, sweatshirt and all.

It's my new favorite article of clothing. Whenever it loses Mario's scent, I wash it before spraying his cologne over it again. Yeah, I've turned into *that* girl. I really can't say it's a problem for me. He smells terrific, and I love having a piece of him around when he's off doing his thing.

Things with him are going great. Since the day my insecurities came tumbling out, we've taken things one day at a time. Neither of us are in a rush, and it's allowed me to tackle my fears about everything falling apart.

Overall, he's the best kind of boyfriend I could ask for. Mario loves to tease me, but he's never cruel. We enjoy so many of the same things, I often wonder if I should be creeped out or if it's a testament to our compatibility. He's also a great listener. He's helped me a time or two to cool down when I've been upset at my parents or even Val.

Sure, there have been some growing pains as a couple, but that's expected. His logical mind has a way of finding a solution to everything. And I do mean, *everything*—something I both love and hate. Sometimes a girl just wants to vent. We aren't always looking for a solution. We don't need to be saved all the time.

Lost in my thoughts, I walk into something before I can even make it to the bench I frequent on days like today. Strong hands steady me while my mind races to piece together the familiar scent when he speaks.

"I'm so sorry! I wasn't watching wh—Izzy?"

"Johnny?"

His bright smile fills his face a moment before he wraps me into his frame. The hug is warm and familiar, and I can't help but smile. "How are you?" I ask and step back. "What are you doing here?"

A blush fills his cheeks, and his eyes dart away. "I have a paper I need to write."

My brows raise. When we were talking, he was working in construction. I distinctly remember having a conversation where he expressed no interest in doing more. "You're taking a class?" I ask after my moment of surprise. "I didn't think you wanted to do anything but construction."

He rubs the back of his neck and meets my eyes. His reveal how nervous he is, almost making him shy before he speaks. "Well, you got me thinking. I really do love construction, and I decided I don't want to be the low man on the totem pole."

"That's wonderful, Johnny! I'm really happy for you!"

"Are you seeing someone?" he blurts, his eyes trained on my sweatshirt.

I smile. "I am."

"Is he treating you well?"

"Mario's great—" I freeze when the hair on the back of my neck stands, an eerie sensation that reminds me of when I'm followed.

"What's wrong?" Johnny asks, standing taller as he goes into a protective stance.

I meet his eyes a moment before looking around. "I feel like someone is—"

Missy.

She's standing on the sidewalk, partly covered by an overgrown oleander plant. Her angry eyes are trained on Johnny before sliding to mine. Her lips tip in a sneer, and a shiver runs down my spine.

"Who's that chick?" he asks after following my gaze.

I shift so I can face Johnny but am not exposed with my back to her. "*That* is Mario's ex."

His brows knit. "Ah… bad blood I see. Did Mario cheat with you or something?"

I meet his eyes at the tone in his words. "I wouldn't date a man who I knew was in a relationship," I snap.

Johnny raises his hands. "I'm sorry, I—"

"Look, I need to get back to work. It was nice seeing you." I spit the words out, uncomfortable with the insinuation I would purposely become the other woman. The venom Missy is shooting in my direction sure disagrees. I'm ready to get as far from her as possible. Johnny and I didn't date long, and I know he doesn't know me well, but I'm angry at his words.

Johnny steps forward and cups my face, turning it up to his. "Izzy, I'm sorry." His whispered words are infused with remorse.

I give him a small nod and whisper back my thanks. He pulls me into his large frame for a hug, and I return it. "It really was good to see you. I hope everything works out."

He pulls back and smiles. "Thanks. Mario's a lucky

man. If you need me to remind him, you know how to find me," he says with a wink and walks away.

I wrap my arms around my waist and close my eyes for a moment. The warm sunshine on my face soothes me. It was nice seeing Johnny, and I'm really glad he's decided to work on this next step. He's passionate about what he does, and this will help him go up the ladder hopefully.

"You really are a whore." Missy seethes on my right.

Inhaling through my nose, I keep my eyes shut tight even if I'm sorely tempted to look her in the eye. It's of no use. She's an angry person. I know there must be a good person somewhere in there if Mario dated her for so long. Only, I don't see it.

I can either ignore her or respond. Nothing good will come out of either response. Instead, I decide to dig deep inside me for some compassion. This woman lost Mario. She loves him, and he no longer reciprocates her love.

After another breath of fresh air, I smile brightly at her. "Hi, Missy! It's a beautiful day, isn't it?" I don't bother to stick around for her response. I could have been as nasty to her—she's done it to me plenty—but I chose not to. Not only did I not lower myself to her standards, I managed to walk away.

The cold AC hits my warm face when I enter the library. No one is standing outside my office waiting for help, so I decide to make a quick round of the machines and let them know at Circulation.

I should tell Mario about the incident with Missy. The problem is I don't want to give him more of a reason to be upset with her. I want them to move on, and adding fuel to that fire isn't going to encourage the healing that needs to happen.

By the time I'm stepping off the top floor elevator to check the machines, I'm no closer to deciding what I

172 | A J   R E N E E

should do if anything. When I round the corner, I find
Mario. He's leaning against the wall, one ankle crossed
over the other and his hand running through his hair. To a
bystander he looks bored, but not to me.

His turbulent eyes meet mine in question, and I stop
in my tracks. I try to gauge the situation when it dawns
on me. "Missy." I curse.

Mario pushes off the wall and stands straight, his
body tense and uneasy—the opposite of what I'm used to.
He sucks his lower lip in and chews on it before blowing
out an exasperated breath. "Is there anything you need to
tell me?" he asks, a hard edge to his voice.

I tilt my head to the side. "Well, it kind of depends
on what you seem to think you know."

"No. I know Missy's nasty side. You've never been
that way with me or others. I want to hear your side of the
story, so I can tell her to fuck off. I will admit it doesn't
look good, and it's taking everything in me not to flip
out. Princess, I need to hear it from you."

I nod. He's not exaggerating. His tense body is
vibrating with how upset he is. I close the distance
between us but don't touch him; I can see he doesn't
want it. Fucking Missy. I can only imagine what she told
him.

"I was freezing, so I went outside to thaw. I literally
bumped into Johnny—"

"Paintballing Johnny?"

I nod. "We chatted for a couple minutes. He asked
me if I was seeing anyone, and I told him you. I asked
him what he was doing on campus, and he mentioned he
had a paper to work on. He's tired of being a worker bee
and wants to move up. We saw Missy, who stared
daggers at us. Johnny left, and Missy called me a whore.
Now, what the hell did she say?"

"Did you guys kiss?" he rasps.

My eyes widen and narrow. "No! Why on earth would I kiss him?"

Mario pulls his phone from his pocket and taps on the screen until he pulls up a picture. Johnny and I are inches apart, and he's cupping my face. I sigh with frustration. It's no wonder Mario is about to lose his damn mind.

"Fucking Missy," I mutter and think back to when the picture was taken. "If I remember correctly, that was after I found Missy creeping. Johnny asked who she was, and I told him, to which he stupidly asked if you cheated on her with me. I was mad and disappointed he'd ask, and that—" I nod toward the now-black screen. "That was when he apologized. I'm surprised she didn't also send you a picture of us hugging. You know, because it would have been a nail in my coffin." With a sigh, I look past him. It's no wonder he's so upset. Here I tried being the better person, and she was playing paparazzi to stir trouble.

"Princess," he whispers, and I meet his eyes, the hardness from moments ago now gone. "I'm sorry."

"Don't be. It looks bad. I know I didn't do anything wrong, but I'd question myself too after that picture. This whole time I checked machines, I debated on whether to tell you Missy was being her wonderful self. And here I find you wound up tight, thanks to her stirring the pot." I raise my brow at him with a humorless laugh. "I don't want any more problems. I want her to move on and to stay out of our lives."

Mario wraps his arms around me and pulls me into him. "I want the same thing. I'm sorry I hunted you down. I needed to know immediately what happened, or else it would have festered, and Missy would have won. I'll take care of Missy."

Putting my hands on his chest, I push away from

him. "No! She wants to cause problems. Ignore her."

"I can't ignore that," he says, an incredulous expression on his face. "She's being outright malicious."

I think on it a minute, and an idea forms. "Here." I put my hand out. "Give me your phone."

He unlocks it and gives it to me without question. I see her text and shake my head at the message that accompanied the picture.

Missy: Your new girlfriend is a real winner. I wonder how many other men she's screwing behind your back?

Mario presses his finger under my chin until our eyes meet. "The text was easy to dismiss. It was the picture. I'm sorry I doubted you for a moment." His mouth lowers to mine, a sweet brush against my lips that sends a tingle down my back. After sealing his apology, he unlocks his phone once more. "What are you going to say?"

"Hold on a second," I mutter and stare at the message window.

Mario: Nice picture of Izzy with Johnny.

Turning the phone, I make sure he sees the message before hitting send.

"Hmm..."

"What?"

"It wasn't what I expected for you to send."

I nod. "I understand. She's only trying to tear us apart. That message shows you know who the man is, and you aren't bothered. She didn't succeed in riling you up."

"But it did work..." he mutters and shoves his fingers through his mussed-up hair.

"She doesn't have to know that. Are we okay? I'm sure if we look around we can find Johnny, and you can meet him yourself." Standing straighter, I look him in the eyes. "I have nothing to hide."

He wraps his hand around my neck and tugs me against his chest. He kisses my hair, and I relax. "Thank you," he whispers, and I hold onto him. "I'm sorry she's causing us grief."

"I am too." After a squeeze, I rise to my toes and kiss him. As I deepen the kiss, a noise startles us. We turn, Mario holding me close, and find Johnny.

"Hey," we say in unison and chuckle.

"This must be the lucky guy," Johnny says and offers Mario his hand.

"I am!" Mario steps aside, shakes Johnny's hand, and pulls me into his side.

I introduce the men and can't help the slight awkwardness over the situation. They are both kind to each other, which I appreciate. I'm grateful neither start a pissing match.

"Izzy tells me you're in construction?" Mario asks.

Johnny smiles with pride. "Yeah, I've been doing it for a few years now. Thanks to her, I decided to return to school. I'm hoping it will help me move on up."

Mario nods. "Nice. My dad was a civil engineer in the military, and my grandfather was in construction."

I look up with surprise. This was new information to me. "I didn't know that!"

A shadow crosses Mario's face when he meets my eyes. "Yeah. It was a bit of a sore spot when I didn't follow the family *biz* if you know what I mean." He shrugs, and I can see it clearly bothers him still.

Johnny laughs without humor. "My pops didn't understand why I would go into construction. Not when I could move into his security company with the opportunity to take over in a few years."

"I didn't know that either!"

Johnny looks between me and Mario. "Well, babe— sorry!" He says the latter to Mario before continuing.

"Izzy, we only had the one date."

Mario squeezes me at the sad tone in Johnny's voice.

"I'm sorry."

"Does he make you happy?" Johnny asks, ignoring the fact that Mario is right here.

I nod and smile at Mario before telling Johnny, "Yes. I'm really happy—"

"Then you have nothing to apologize for. We didn't work out. It happens. You're a real sweetheart, Izzy. Life's too short to be with the wrong person." His tone is serious and unlike the happy and easygoing man I dated briefly. "Well, I really do need to finish working on this paper. It was nice meeting you, Mario. You've got a great one, and I wish you both all the best!"

The two of them shake hands, and I hug him goodbye. We watch Johnny walk down the hall toward the row of desks students prefer on this quiet floor. Once he's out of view, Mario wraps his arm around my shoulders and guides me to the elevator.

"He seems like a nice guy," he says as the doors close behind us.

"From the little time I spent with him, yeah, he is."

CHAPTER 22

I should thank Missy, but I'm not going to because the woman doesn't deserve any more of my time. After the incident with Johnny three months ago, she tried to stir trouble for Mario and me another three times. If only she knew her antics have only pushed Mario and me closer together. Our communication has become stronger thanks to her.

The most entertaining of the events was when Val twisted her ankle during finals. No, it wasn't funny at all, especially when we learned Val had a hairline fracture from her fall. I wasn't on campus and Mason wasn't available to help her out. Mario, on the other hand, was at work. He met Val, who was a mess, and gave her a piggyback ride. At first he tried carrying her, but she didn't want to draw any more attention to herself. He put her in his car and sat with her at the ER until Mason arrived.

Thanks to Missy, I got a series of pictures that looked rather compromising. Unbeknownst to her, I knew about Mario being with Val. Hell, I'm the one who asked him to step in. My favorite picture was of Mario holding

Val when they stood by his car. Val's leg was popped back thanks to her injury, but I must admit how romantic the moment looked.

I'm still not sure how the hell she got a hold of my cell number. After the last incident, we agreed to block her from our lives. We allowed her enough power over our dating life, and now the only in she ever got was if she chose to come out of the shadows in person. I think she has a career ahead of her as a paparazzo.

Pushing aside my thoughts of Missy, I check the duffle bag on my bed. Mario has instructed me to pack a variety of things, and I must admit, I'm really confused as to what he has planned. Today is our six-month anniversary, which is not long at all, but it feels like we've been together much longer. This bag has received a lot of mileage. If I'm not at his place, he's here at mine. Val and I only see each other in passing, girls' nights, or when we do double dates.

Things between her and Mason are going well, and she's finally relaxing. It's been way too long for her, and it makes me giddy to see her happy.

"Are you ready for today?" Val asks, a grin brightening her face.

"I can't believe you won't tell me what he has planned!"

She laughs. "Nope. It's brilliant, and he came up with it all on his own."

A thought occurs to me, and I freeze. "He's not proposing, is he?"

Val's brows raise, and she steps farther into the room. "Honey, you two haven't even admitted you're in love with one another."

I blow out a breath and realize how stupid my question was. "You're right. I don't even know why I thought that."

"Because you love him and want to marry him and have his babies?" Val says with a straight face.

"I do, but we should probably stick to that order."

"Why haven't you guys said 'I love you'?"

I shrug. "I guess I'm just nervous. I'm pretty sure he feels the same way."

"Chicken shits, both of you," she says with a shake of her head.

"Yup! It'll probably slip out soon. I've almost said it a hundred times by now."

A knock sounds from down the hall, and Val steps forward. "Sounds like your Prince Charming has arrived. Go let him in while I double-check your bag."

After checking the peep hole, I let him in as I grin. "Hi, baby!"

He smiles and steps into me. I'm wrapped into him as his lips descend on mine. A thud sounds at my feet, and we pull back.

Val laughs before pointing at the bag. "She has everything you asked for."

"Great, thanks for your help on this, Val."

"Go have fun, you crazy kids!" She winks, and Mario grabs my bag.

We call out a quick goodbye while she effectively shoves us out the apartment. I'm not sure if I should be concerned or amused. One thing is for sure. I'm really excited for whatever he's planned.

***

"You're not going to tell me, are you?"

"Nope."

"You're mean!" I cross my arms over my chest in an exaggerated pout.

Mario laughs and pulls my hand free, so he can thread his fingers in mine. The touch makes my lips twitch with the need to smile. There are times he aggravates me, but it's hard to stay mad at him for long. Then again, he hasn't ever done anything truly horrible. Annoying? Most definitely. But never unforgivable.

I lean forward to turn up the music and relax in our companionable silence. This is how things are with us. Comfortable and easy. Passionate and breathtaking. Beautiful and loving.

I'm head over heels in love with him. He hasn't heard it from me yet but soon… Soon I'll let him in on my not-so-secret secret. People always say when you're with the right person you just *know*. I didn't. My fears completely blinded me. If they hadn't, I would have known immediately Mario is different from the other men.

He balances me and finds a way to be this silent strength when I don't realize I need it. He's become my best friend in addition to lover. We have this amazing, beautiful package I could have missed out on if I'd have let my fear win.

I'm pulled from my thoughts when he parks near my favorite café. "Oh! You're forgiven!" I chuckle, tossing him a smile before hurrying out of the car. I've already had my morning coffee, but a hot chocolate sounds divine.

He chuckles, and we meet behind the car. "I didn't realize I'd done anything wrong."

I shrug in reply and look both ways before crossing. I pull on his hand and jog across the street, but he stops us on the sidewalk. One arm bands around my waist, and the other cups my neck. His mouth crashes into mine. I grab handfuls of fabric. The kiss is scorching and leaves me desperate for more.

One moment I'm considering wrapping my legs around his waist, and the next I'm wobbling over. Mario grins and tugs on my hand, aware of the fact he's made my brain mush with only a kiss.

I whimper at his back. "Jerk face!"

I can't help my smile when he chuckles without turning around. We order our drinks and sit in a booth. Our thighs touch hip to knee, and his free arm is around my shoulders, holding me close.

"This is nice. I love their hot chocolate."

"I should hope so. You came here every day during the winter."

It's true, and I have nothing to apologize for, so I simply shrug. Life is too short to drink bad hot chocolate.

Mario excuses himself and goes to the counter. I look at my phone and find a text from Val.

Val: Have fun today. Make sure to relax!

I smile to myself and jump when something is put under my nose. After a second glance, my eyes dart up to Mario's smiling ones.

"Happy six months, princess!"

I take the rose from his hand and smell it. "Thanks, baby!" The sweet gesture warms my heart.

"Thank you for giving us a chance. Now, drink up, we have places to go, and I'm craving peach cobbler from the diner."

I raise my brows and toss back the last bit of my hot chocolate. "Let's get my pregnant man his pie."

He tickles me, and I curl into myself with laughter. "You think you're funny?"

"Yes!" I say breathless a moment later.

The diner isn't far, so we walk there, and he orders a slice of pie. He feeds me a couple bites, but I'm full from the oatmeal I ate earlier. I didn't know he planned to bring us to the café or diner, or I would've waited.

The waitress brings us the bill, and I notice a silent exchange between them before she clears the table. I raise my brow in question, but he only smiles.

"Our next stop," he says with a bit of hesitation. "Val warned me you might not be happy about it. I would really like you to bear with me and keep an open mind."

Before I can reply, the waitress returns. She winks at me and presents me with a red rose. "You've got a keeper."

I meet Mario's eyes and see his sweet smile. I smell the rose and set it next to my other one. "Are you trying to butter me up for whatever I won't be happy about?"

"No. I mean yes, if it means you won't be pissed at me later?"

I laugh at him. "The flowers are working, but with how you're making it sound, I think you might need to get more."

"Well, keep an open mind, okay?"

I narrow my eyes at him. "I'll try." What's he got planned? At least Val confirmed it wasn't a proposal.

As we drive toward the other side of town, my nerves kick in. I don't come out this way often, and it's been almost a year since I have. Mario's thumb has been drawing invisible circles on my hand with intermittent sweet kisses on my fingers.

I've been partly paying attention to him as he informs me his favorite band is coming back into town. Taking in the familiar area, I try to figure out why I recognize it. My stomach dips low into my belly when the light bulb finally turns on.

"Oh, hell no!"

"Izzy, please keep an open mind," he asks calmly.

"I didn't pack for this, and I refuse to ruin my outfit," I snap like a spoiled brat.

Mario chuckles. "Val made sure to—"

"I'm going to kill her!"

Freeing my hand, I cross my arms and look around the parking lot. Today is cooler than the hot day I'd met Johnny so long ago. The car stops moving, and the engine shuts off.

Mario releases my seatbelt and drags me onto his lap. "Princess, I promise this will be fun."

"Liar! Those damn paintballs hurt like a motherfucker!"

"I'll protect you. We'll work as a team," he says and cups my cheek.

Meeting his eyes, I sigh. "I was black and blue for weeks, Mario."

"Maybe you should shoot better."

My brows knit together, and I smack his arm. "Don't be a—"

Mario laughs, a full belly one that jostles me around. "I'm teasing, princess. Will you please do this for me?"

Looking away, I stare at the trailer and course behind it. When I came here with Johnny, I didn't know what to expect. This time, I do. Those players can be pricks, and right now I have my annoyance driving me. I'll get hit again, but this time I'll get some retribution.

"Fine."

He tilts his head and captures my lips in his, his fingers running through my hair and cupping it at the base of my neck. My toes curl at the intensity, and I consider pushing his seat back and finding a whole other game to play with Mario. One that can get dirty but doesn't involve bruises.

CHAPTER 23

"You owe me a massage and wine."

He chuckles and tosses our bags into the trunk. "Can I get a massage too?"

I snort. "Aww, are you hurting?"

Mario closes the trunk and walks me to the passenger door. "Did you have fun?" he asks, ignoring my question.

With a roll of my eyes, I shrug. "I suppose."

"Did I not protect you and work with you as a team?"

"Maybe?"

He shakes his head and smiles down at me. "If it's any consolation, I have quite a few bruises already."

My eyes soften. "I don't want you hurting." I sigh. "I enjoyed myself. I played better than last time, and I think my teammate was sexy as hell out there." My fingers curl into the jeans he's changed into.

"Only out there?" he asks before pressing me against the car.

When our kiss ends, he opens the door, and I find a rose on my seat. I breathe in the fragrance and add it to the others as Mario closes my door. This anniversary is going differently than I expected, and I'm on the verge of blurting my first "I love you."

Inside, I changed from the camo Val packed into a skirt and blouse. I used the baby wipes I found in my bag to clean up and reapplied deodorant and perfume. I'm thankful I decided not to wear any makeup that morning. I'm already a hot mess since I couldn't take a shower after the sweaty game.

"Are you hungry?" Mario asks after we sit in the car a bit.

"Yeah, I'm starved."

"Good, I have a place in mind."

"I'm sure you do," I smirk. The roses sit on my lap, and I can't help myself from running my fingertips over their soft petals. "Will I get a hint at least?"

"No."

When I spot the familiar sign, I groan. I remain frozen, staring at the building until Mario opens my door and offers his hand. "Really? Here? *This* is where you want to eat on our anniversary?"

"Yup. Come on, princess."

Walking next to him, I look between Mario, the restaurant, and our interlocked fingers. There are thousands of restaurants in this town, and he brings me to the one Italian restaurant I could have happily avoided for the rest of my life: the place Brad the Chump dumped me with the bill. I'm starting to question Mario's intentions today. Did he hit his head?

Mario gives the hostess the name for our reservation, and we are seated immediately. On the table is another rose. I smile and bring it to my nose after mouthing my thank you. Mario waits patiently while I choose my meal. He encourages me to pick a wine for us to share. We share pleasant conversation and people-watch. It's relaxing, sweet, and romantic as hell. Lunch is great.

"Normally I'd encourage you to order a dessert, but there's somewhere else I planned to take you."

I nod, and he grabs my hand. His relaxed posture becomes rigid, and I can't help but get nervous.

"There's something I've needed to tell you for a while, and—" He blows out a breath and rubs his neck with his free hand.

My heart hammers in my chest as I begin to worry. "Mario?"

"I didn't realize I'd been going through the motions, doing what was expected and saying things I didn't mean. When we spoke the first time in the breakroom, you captured me in your web. I didn't know how to undo the mess I'd created in my life. I should have left Missy earlier for a variety of reasons, but mostly because she wasn't the woman I wanted. You were. You are. I'm so lucky to call you my girlfriend, Izabella Rae. I guess what I'm trying to say and completely fumbling is that I'm madly in love with you."

Warm tears trickle down my cheeks, and my heart expands, filling my chest with so much love it wants to burst. "I love you too!" I grin and wipe my face as I laugh. Mario closes the distance between us and kisses me.

"I love you so damn much," he whispers against my lips between kisses.

A throat clears, and we look up into the embarrassed waitress's face. "Sorry, you asked for the bill?"

"Ah, yes." Mario grabs the black folder and returns to his seat with a new lightness to him that I'm sure mirrors my own. "Is this my cue to exit, so you can pay?" he teases and hands the folder back to the waitress when she walks by.

I grab the napkin off my lap and toss it at his head. Mario catches it before it connects, and he laughs. "Don't be a jerk after your sweet speech."

"Did you enjoy your lunch?" he asks, all traces of humor gone.

"Very much. Telling me you love me has been the best part of this whole crazy day."

"Izzy, you deserve to be wined and dined. You're the easiest person to love, and I'm so damn lucky to have you."

"Take me home."

His eyes darken with desire, and warmth spreads through my body. I want this man, but more than anything, I love him. I need to show him with my touch how deep my love goes. My hands itch with the need to peel off his clothes, to caress and kiss every inch of skin I reveal. I—

"Izzy, princess, you're killing me here." His voice is deep, and I hear how badly he wants me.

"Take me home."

"Not yet. Soon, I promise. Very soon."

Thankfully, the waitress returns then with his card and receipt. He scribbles away and tosses it on the table before offering me his hand. I take it without question, and we nearly run out of the restaurant with my rose in hand.

The barely restrained passion between us threatens to burst free. I'm not one for sex in public, but I need Mario between my legs, buried so deep inside me we won't be able to tell where one begins and the other ends. Right this moment, as he rushes me into his car, I consider the real possibility of being taken where anyone might see.

Lost in my fog of passion, I don't remember Mario helping me into his car or even the sound of the door closing. I lean over as he turns the key, the engine coming to life. Grazing my lips over his ear, I hear his harsh gasp.

"Princess, please," he begs.

Running my hand up his thigh, I find him hard and ready. "Yes?"

Our next kiss is wild and needy. Our teeth clink and nip. Our hands roam, caress, and dig into flesh. It's hot and sexy, and I'm past the point of thinking.

Mario cups my face and presses kisses all over it. "Izzy, princess, not here."

His voice sounds tortured to my ears. Hearing the pain in his words is a bucket of ice-cold water. I'm confused and disoriented. And hurt. "Sorry, I—um—I—" I stop and pull free from him. Once I'm seated in my chair, I find it hard to look at him. I blink away the cloudiness from my eyes. All I hear in the hot car is our harsh breaths. If his heart is anything like mine, it's racing, trying to escape the confines of his ribs.

He tells me he loves me, and I jump all over him. There's nothing out there that says sex succeeds a declaration of love. My body warms with embarrassment. I want to curl up and pretend I didn't just get rejected by my boyfriend, someone I love and adore. Maybe it's for the best. I was two seconds from either going down on him in this parking lot or riding him until everyone heard us come. I'm not really sure which one. Needing to focus on something else, I straighten my clothes and pull the seatbelt until it clicks.

"Hey?" he whispers after a few minutes.

I shake my head, refusing to meet his eyes. We've never experienced an awkward silence. Not until now. What on earth is wrong with me?

Mario turns up the AC, and the blast of cool air blows my hair back. He gives me the space I clearly need and begins to drive. I watch the buildings go by as I ignore the ache in my heart, in my breasts, and between my legs.

After a few miles, he threads his fingers with mine and sets it on his thigh. No words. Only a simple connection and I release a breath I didn't realize I held. This man drives me crazy. But more than that, he's the calm in my storm, soothing and handling me like the scared fillies I've read about in my romance novels. I always thought the comparison was dumb, but it's exactly how Mario treats me. He sees past my walls and gives me exactly what I need.

When he parks the car sometime later, I'm surprised to find us at the café once again. "Why are we here?" I whisper when he cuts the engine.

He presses his lips on my hand and smiles. "For dessert."

His smile doesn't reach his eyes, and I know it's my fault. All because I couldn't keep my hands to myself. I nod and open my door, trying to release my hand from his, but he won't let go. I'm pulled toward him. His free hand cups my face, and his thumb caresses the apple to my cheek.

"I love you so damn much, Izabella." The brush of his lips on mine is soft and sweet. Another piece of me sighs, coming back from the turbulent emotions that spiraled me out of control.

I smile when he pulls back. "I love you too."

"Welcome back, you two," the café owner calls out when we enter.

Mario wraps his arm around my shoulders and kisses my hair. "Thanks! Can we have a brownie sundae?"

He escorts me to the booth from earlier and returns to pay. While I wait, I close my eyes and vow to turn today around. My phone vibrates next to me, and I notice I've missed a few texts. All but one is from Mario.

Val: Enjoy your day. He's a keeper.

I close the text without replying and see Mario has

190 | AJ RENEE

sent an image, a series of them. I cover my mouth as they load. Mario. Naked. Well, mostly naked. Each picture exposes a sliver of him except for his goods.

Another text comes in from Mario, and I see it's a selfie we took earlier in the day. On it he's written the date in the corner and drawn a heart around our heads. I can't help but chuckle at the sweet and silly image.

"What's so funny?" he asks, jarring me back and placing our brownie sundae on the table.

I turn my screen and show him. He wipes his brow in exaggeration. "For a second there, I thought you were laughing at my nakedness." He winks and presents another red rose.

This man has pulled all the stops. When did he drop off the roses for today? We were together until midnight before he picked me up this morning. "How did you manage all this?" I ask.

Mario sits to my right and offers me a spoon. "I'll never show my hand."

"That's not all you won't show," I mumble, still frustrated with his rejection.

He sets down the spoon, lays his arm behind me across the booth, and turns. I freeze, my eyes on the delicious-looking bowl on the table. Crap, he wasn't supposed to hear that.

His free hand cups the side of my neck, my pulse thumping wildly against his palm. He leans forward, and his nose runs up my skin until his lips brush my ear. The wisps of breath send bolts of lightning down my body to my sex.

"The thought alone of peeling your clothes off has me hard and throbbing. My control is barely hanging on, and by the way your heart is racing, I know you feel the same way. There is plenty of time for show-and-tell. No way in hell am I rejecting you, but it'd be nice if I can shower you with more than sexual release."

He brushes his lips over mine before turning to our dessert. I pant, short little puffs of air slipping from my mouth at his brief kiss. Logically and emotionally his words have touched me, but hot damn!

Is this what a bitch in heat feels like?

Mario scoops ice cream onto his spoon and brings it to my lips. "Open up. It will help you cool down."

Doing as he asks, I don't miss the small growl in his throat when my lips wrap around the metal spoon. I can't speak. I nod and grab my own spoon before we enjoy our treat in silence. Between the cold ice cream and our mini time-out, we manage to collect ourselves.

He pushes the bowl toward me. "You can have the last bite."

I smile. "Thanks."

I'm stuffed and happy to sit here talking and people-watching with him. We talk about our day and the things each of us enjoyed and hated about paintballing. I'm not surprised it wasn't his first time, but I'm glad he didn't abandon me to go play G.I. Joe. When I shiver against him, he orders me a hot chocolate. How did I get so lucky?

He slides the mug toward me and pulls me into him. "I have some news I want to tell you." I meet his eyes, and he continues. "I heard back from Cheryl," he says, referring to the head of the Reference Department.

"Yeah? And what did she say?"

"I got the internship!"

A squeal of glee slips free as I wrap my arms around him. "That's awesome! Congratulations!"

He chuckles. "Thank you!"

"We need to celebrate!" A thought occurs to me, and I still. "Wait, is that part of what today has been all about? Why didn't you tell me immediately?"

"No, today has been about *us*. Although, I've managed to screw it up by upsetting you," he says with a sad smile.

Leaning into him, I press my lips to his. "Today has been wonderful. It's not your fault I can't keep my hands to myself... or wait, it *is* your fault. Quit being so hot!"

"I'll get right on that," he says with a straight face and chuckles.

"When did you find out about the internship?"

He picks at the napkin on the table and side-eyes me. "Wednesday?"

My mouth opens and closes. "Wednesday? Today is Saturday. Wh—" I quiet mid-question and stare at him.

"I'd already set things in motion for today. I didn't want it to overshadow our anniversary."

"Overshadow our anniversary? With acceptance into the internship you've been dying for?" I shake my head at him. "I love you, but you're an idiot."

"Gee, thanks."

"Baby, your accomplishment should never feel like something that would overshadow us. I'm sad you'd think that."

"I wanted today to be perfect for you... for us. You deserve so much happiness. Missy hasn't made this easy for us either."

I smile. "Silly man, I *am* happy! As far as Missy? I feel sorry for her. She had you and lost you. You're a really good man. Will you take me home now?"

"And you're a really good woman." Mario looks at the time and slides out of the booth. "We have one last stop and then I'll take you home. Okay?"

"Only if you promise to make love to me when we do get home."

He gathers me in his arms, and the kiss is sweet, tender, and filled with so much love, tears pool behind my lids. "Promise."

CHAPTER 24

"Enzo's? Are they even open yet?" I ask as we walk toward their tinted front door.

Mario grins. "I may have called in a favor."

I laugh. "You have someone you can call for favors at Enzo's?"

"I know people!"

Before I can ask him more on the matter, he escorts me inside where one lone bartender is stocking supplies. The man winks at us and returns to his task. Chairs are upside down on tables, save for one table and two chairs. A single candle is lit in the center next to a vase nearly overfilled with roses.

"Oh!" I gasp in surprise.

Mario's lips press against my ear. "Happy Anniversary, beautiful." He helps me into my chair and excuses himself. I watch him stroll to the bar and exchange a few words with the man. Returning my attention to our table, I grab the vase and pull the flowers toward me. Breathing them in, I smile. My man is so damn romantic!

"I got you the house pinot noir," Mario tells me,

placing a glass of red wine in front of me before sitting beside me.

"Thank you. For all of this." I lean forward and kiss him.

"Thank you for giving us a shot, for not running away when Missy tried her hardest to split us up."

I raise my glass of wine to his pint of beer. "To love, happiness, and lots of sex."

Mario snorts, and the beer sloshes over the side of his glass. "To the crazy, smart, and beautiful woman I want a future with."

I dig my teeth into my lip and set the glass down without drinking. I grab him by the back of his neck and pull him forward. Our lips meet, and I pour all the passion and love I have for him into another kiss, all the while mentally reminding myself to not lose control like before.

"I love you."

"I love you too."

After a sip of the wine, I tilt my head to the side. "You put a lot of thought and work into today."

"I did."

"Thank you."

Mario shakes his head. "There's no reason to thank me. I wanted today to be special. Something to celebrate us, a way to put the past behind us."

There is something about the way he's looking at me. I sip more wine and think about the day. He surprised me with roses at every turn, took me to the café, diner, paintballing, lunch at the Italian restaurant, the café... and now we're at Enzo's. It's all familiar, and yet—

I gasp and narrow my eyes at him. "Put the past behind us?"

He smirks as he nods. "Mhmm," he says and takes a deep pull of his beer.

"For our six-month anniversary, you brought us to places I went with other dates? Why?" I'm completely shocked and intrigued by this revelation. It's odd that any person would purposely make a day of returning to the scene of the crime.

Mario scoots closer, and my knees tuck in between his. His warm hands grab one of mine from my lap. "Izzy, it's no secret you went on some awful dates before we became a couple."

"Gee, thanks!" I say, mimicking his tone from earlier.

He chuckles and brings my hand to his mouth. "Our first kiss was a reenactment of one of those bad dates. What better way to celebrate us than to recreate them, erasing the bad memories by overriding them with ones of us?"

My mouth forms an O, and if possible, I'm left speechless. I think over all the details of our day and realize I'll remember them more than any of those men or the dates I went on with them. Mario's loving gesture is easily the best gift I've ever been given.

"Say something," he whispers.

I smile and put my free hand on our three. Now when I think of the café, I'll remember the surprise and happiness Mario's first rose filled me with. And I'm not as battered and bruised from today's paintball game as I was with Johnny's.

I burst into a fit of laughter and Mario asks, "What?"

"The mostly naked pictures you sent me earlier? Were those to replace Robert's?"

Mario growls. "You don't know how sick that text I saw made me. I was still with Missy, and it wasn't my place to say anything. I hated it. It's after my strong reaction when I found myself reevaluating my relationship."

"I didn't know that," I whisper, recalling the way he grunted a reply and left the breakroom. I figured it was awkward for him but not this. It's another piece of information I didn't know. There is so much more to Mario than I ever realized, and clearly his thoughtfulness has no bounds.

He nods. "I took what I could remember and asked Val for help on other details. You mentioned being unlucky in love, and I thought this was a great way to give you happy memories. At least I hope it's what I've done."

I grin. "So happy!"

"Great, because I've never been happier. Well, maybe that's not true…"

My heart begins to sink, but before it can hit the ground, Mario is kneeling at my feet with a black gift box in his hand. I stare at him in shock. Val told me this wasn't a proposal. I'm going to kick her ass! What is wrong with him? We've only been together six months! My heart races, and I tremble, goose bumps raising the skin on my arms. Pure panic hits me in a split second.

"There is one thing that would make me even happier," he says before lifting the lid to the box. "Will you move in with me?"

My eyes flick between his eyes, mouth, and the silver key sitting on a pillow of tissue paper. What did he say?

"I said, will you move in with me?" he repeats, this time with less confidence as I realize I've spoken the words out loud.

Move in with Mario?

Meeting his eyes, all I see is love. "Are you sure? Is this not too soon?" My voice waivers, excitement and fear warring within me.

He smiles. "You feel like home, and I hate being

apart from you."

Taking a deep breath, I remind myself this is Mario. He spent the entire day erasing bad memories and declaring his love. "You feel like home too." My words slip free, and a wave of calm washes over me. We spend most of our free time together. He's my future and what a better way to show that than taking this step.

"Yes!" My hand trembles as I palm the key. It's standard size and weight, and the cold metal warms in my hand. The significance of this moment is not lost on me. Imaginary chains break, and I realize "I'm no longer unlucky in love."

"No, princess, you're not." Mario grins and gathers me into his arms. "How about we finish this drink, and I'll take you to our place where I can show you exactly how *lucky* in love we are?"

ABOUT THE AUTHOR

AJ Renee grew up in a military family and moved around until her family settled in Florida. She graduated from the University of Central Florida with a M.S. in Criminal Justice and a B.S. in Psychology. She currently resides in Illinois and spends her time with her Air Force husband, three young daughters, dog, and cat. She loves to travel and see family and friends whenever she gets a chance. She has a love of music, movies, and anything that can make her laugh. AJ believes in reading books with humor and mystery that end in a happily ever after to help ease our minds and hearts of life's daily struggles.

To stay up to date on new releases, go to www.AJRenee.com.

ALSO BY AJ RENEE

ST. FLEUR SERIES:

Widower's Aura

Always Mine

Duplicity

No Going Back

Taxed by Love

OTHER TITLES:

Finding Love at the Falls… (Short Story)

Fractured Fairytales Book One

Beauty Unmasked

Winter's Surprise

A Deadly World: Vampires in Paris

Billionaires Club

Unlucky in Love

Made in the USA
Monee, IL
13 January 2020